Treasured Legacies

A MARY O'REILLY PARANORMAL MYSTERY

(Book Twelve)

by

Terri Reid

"...You have crossed the chasm, deep and wide—

Why build you the bridge at the eventide?"

The builder lifted his old gray head:

"Good friend, in the path I have come," he said,

"There followeth after me today

A youth whose feet must pass this way.

This chasm that has been naught to me

To that fair-haired youth may a pitfall be.

He, too, must cross in the twilight dim;

Good friend, I am building the bridge for him."

The Bridge Builder - Will Allen Dromgoole

This book is dedicated to my parents, Richard and Virginia Onines, whose legacy of hard-work, compassion, love and encouragement has touched countless lives. And whose patient and tireless bridge-building has saved many weary travelers.

Terri Reid

TREASURED LEGACIES – A MARY O'REILLY
PARANORMAL MYSTERY

by

Terri Reid

The author would like to thank all those who have contributed to the creation of this book: Richard Reid, Sarah Powers, Richard Onines, Virginia Onines, Denise Carpenter, Juliette Wilson and Cyndy Ranzau.

Prologue

The wind rushed through the tops of the trees, sending a shower of gold and red leaves down onto the driveway between the back porch and the barnyard. Dale Johnson mentally added raking the back yard to his ever growing list of things to do as he lifted the collar of his barn coat against the cold wind and made his way to the calf pen.

His children, two sons and a daughter, had taken over most of the running of the farm now that he was nearing retirement, but there were a few things he still enjoyed doing and taking care of the calves was one of them. He turned on the spigot that filled the trough with cold water and then walked over to the barn to scoop grain into buckets. He filled two five-gallon pails and carried them back to the pen, letting himself into the fenced-in area. He dumped the grain into the smaller buckets and then turned to greet the curious animals. The calves came over to him, pushing their soft velvet noses into his hand for the small pieces of apple he carried in his coat pocket. "Hey there, Buster," he laughed at a particularly aggressive bull calf. "How about sharing with the others?"

The little calf just nosed in further, trying to investigate Dale's pocket, and left a smear of saliva across the front of the canvas coat. "There you go, making a mess," Dale laughed. "What in the world is the missus going to say when she sees this?"

He patted the calf on the head, gently pushed it on its way, picked up the empty buckets and moved to turn off the spigot. As he shut off the water, he paused and looked carefully at the grain bin across the yard from him. The small door at the bottom of one of the grain silos was open. Shaking his head, he let himself out of the pen, put the buckets on the ground and walked over to the 80-foot-tall concrete silo.

The field corn harvest was just beginning; the combines were out in the fields, harvesting the grain and dumping it into the backs of the waiting trucks. Most of the silos on the farm were already filled with oats or silage, but the few remaining silos closest to the barn were used for corn storage.

Dale grabbed hold of the iron hatch and pulled the door open the rest of the way. He peered inside, not wanting to risk trapping someone inside the huge cylinder. Stepping through the hatchway, about two feet above the ground, he let his eyes adjust to the dimness of the interior and then looked around. The silo had been recently cleaned and now awaited the new harvest's bounty. The silo was made up of layers of cement tiles and steel hoops stacked one above the other, to the height needed for storage. He looked up and could only see a pinpoint of light where the top of the silo opened for the grain to be poured in through a series of augers on the outside of the building.

"I'll have to have a talk with the kids," he muttered. "Be a damn shame if part of the harvest came spilling out all over the ground because someone was careless. They should know better."

He grabbed hold of the silo wall and bent over to exit the hatchway. Hearing a noise just outside, he started to turn, but a solid blow to the back of his head had him reeling and falling back into the interior of the silo. He looked up and once again could see the pinpoint of light, but then everything went black.

Was it raining outside? Dale wondered as he woke up. It was dark and he could hear the sound of rain hitting the roof. Suddenly, he was pelted with something small and hard. He opened his eyes and sat up, nearly fainting in the process. His head was pounding. *What the hell happened?*

He was pelted again and realized he was being hit with small pieces of corn. His stomach twisted and his heart pounded. He wasn't in his house; he was in the grain silo!

Struggling to his feet, he lurched to the wall and found the hatch. He found the latch and pushed, but it was stuck fast. Pounding on it, bloodying his hands, he tried again and again to unlatch the door.

The grain was now being emptied into the silo at a rapid rate. Dust from the corn was filling the interior and Dale coughed as he continued to fight with the door. "Help me," he yelled, "I'm caught in here!"

The roar of the auger and the dump truck drowned out his voice, but he kept calling out and pounding on the metal door. "I'm in here," he screamed, as the grain filled the bottom of the silo, first covering his feet, then his knees, his hips and finally, it was waist high.

He thought about his family, especially his wife, who would be waiting supper for him. He thought about his grandkids, who he'd never see grow up. He thought about his kids and prayed they wouldn't blame themselves for the accident. Finally, as the grain moved up past his chin, he took a final deep breath and thought about dying.

Chapter One

Mary's cell phone rang as Bradley left their bedroom to help Clarissa. Mary was in bed, by order of her doctor, after her encounter with a serial killer. She reached over and picked up the phone. "Hello?"

"May I speak with Mary Alden please?"

"This is Mary Alden," Mary replied with a little smile as she repeated her fairly new last name.

"Hello, Mary, this is Freeport Hospital with your lab results," the woman on the other end said. "There is no internal bleeding, but you did have a minor concussion. You can take acetaminophen, but nothing stronger, and no ibuprofen because of your condition."

"My condition?" Mary asked, worried.

"Oh, you did know you are pregnant, didn't you?" the nurse said.

Mary sat up straight. "I'm sorry, could you please repeat that?"

"You did know you are pregnant?" she repeated.

Shaking her head, Mary took a deep shuddering breath. "No. No, I didn't know that," she said. "And how do you know? I didn't ask to be tested… I never even considered…"

"When we do blood work in the Emergency Room, we routinely screen for pregnancy in case any procedures that might be dangerous for the baby are suggested. You don't have to ask for it."

"But, are you sure?" Mary asked. "That I'm still…you know…"

For some reason she couldn't bring herself to say the word.

"Pregnant," the nurse stated. "Well, a positive indicator on a pregnancy test means that you have a hormone called human chorionic gonadotropin or hCG in your bloodstream. That hormone is released by your placenta soon after fertilization. The hormone levels increase as the pregnancy increases. However, considering what happened to you during the assault, I can't guarantee that you are still pregnant. I can only tell you that there are appropriate hormone levels in your system to indicate a positive test result."

"So, what do I do?" Mary asked.

"I can't give you medical advice," she said. "But I would suggest you go see your OB/GYN before you do anything else."

"Thanks, that's a good idea," Mary replied with a sigh.

"And be positive and happy," the nurse added. "Endorphins are good for the baby."

"I will," Mary said, a smile on her face. "Thank you."

She hung up the phone, lay back against the pillows and tentatively placed her hands on her abdomen. "Oh, please be okay," she whispered, running her hands slowly up and down her sides.

"Hey, who was on the phone?" Bradley asked, carrying in a plate of cookies and a glass of milk.

Mary dropped her hands to the bed, took a deep breath and pasted a smile on her face. "The hospital," she said.

"Is everything okay?" he asked, placing the food down on the nightstand and sitting next to her.

"I'm …" she began, then stopped. *He really doesn't need any more stress*, she decided. *Besides, until I know for sure, there isn't really anything to tell.*

"I have a minor concussion, but there is no internal bleeding," she said. "And I can have acetaminophen for pain."

"That's it?" he asked.

Mary shrugged. "She told me to have a follow-up with my doctor."

"And when are you going to set that up?" he asked, raising one eyebrow.

Smiling at him, she rolled her eyes. "I'll call her first thing Monday morning, okay?"

"Okay," he replied, meeting her eyes. "Now, tell me what happened today."

Confused, she shook her head and quickly winced in pain. "Ouch," she said, pausing for a moment. "When today?"

"Today between when you came home from shopping and when you went to the hospital in an ambulance."

"Oh, that today," she replied meekly, biting her lower lip and looking down at the blankets on the bed. Finally, she looked up at him, met his eyes and tried as best she could to lie. "I slipped on some paper and cracked my head on the butcher block counter," she said. "Clumsy me."

He placed a hand on either side of her and leaned close, kissing her nose. "Good try," he said. "But I've learned that lying is not one of your strengths. So, why don't you fill me in on the details?"

"It's really not that important," she said, slipping her arms around his neck.

He scooted closer to her and placed his forehead lightly against hers. "Mary, we are going to be doing this parenting thing together, right?" he asked. "And if we withhold information from each other, I can't see it helping anyone."

"I don't want to be a snitch," she said softly. "I don't want her to think I'm running to you with every little thing she's done wrong."

"But you haven't, have you?" he asked. "She's been testing you since we got back from our honeymoon and you've tried to deal with it, on your own."

"You were busy with work," she explained, shrugging slightly. "I didn't want to bother you."

He sighed deeply and shook his head. "Yeah, I was busy. But I need to remember I'm a husband and a dad now," he said. "We are all going to have to adjust to being a family."

She placed her head on his shoulder and exhaled softly. "Maybe she's just adjusting too," she said.

"And maybe she's angry and scared," he replied. "Maybe she needs more help than we can give her. Maybe her acting out is really a cry for help."

A tear slipped down Mary's cheek. "I'm so sorry, Bradley," she whispered. "I really tried to do what I thought was right, what was best. I tried to show her I love her…"

He leaned back and put a hand under her chin, gently lifting her face so he could see her. Tracks of tears marked her cheeks and more overflowed from her eyes. "Darling, this is not your fault," he said.

"But I'm her mother," Mary replied with a stammer. "I should be able to reach her, help her."

"No," he said, placing a kiss on her cheek and then, leaning across her to the nightstand, pulled some tissues from the box and handed them to her. "Now, wipe your eyes and listen to me."

Blowing into the tissues, she nodded.

"If Clarissa were running a high fever or had fallen down and broken her arm, we wouldn't think twice about bringing her to a doctor, right?" he asked.

She nodded.

"And you wouldn't think you had failed her if you couldn't put a cast on her arm or write her a prescription for antibiotics, right?"

She nodded again.

"Well, Clarissa has gone through emotional trauma that no child should ever have to live through," he said. "But she did, she survived. However, as she struggled to survive things got broken; trust, self-esteem… I don't know, her whole

10

view of the world is a place that rips everything she loves away from her. She needs help to fix the broken parts."

"Professional help," Mary said. "A counselor?"

"Why don't you call your friend in Chicago, Gracie Williams, the psychologist," Bradley suggested. "And see what she thinks."

Mary nodded. "Okay, I can do that," she said thoughtfully. "Gracie is great."

"Maybe there are some group meetings for kids dealing with issues," he suggested.

"That's a great idea," she said, with a relieved smile. "I just want her to be happy."

He pulled her into his arms and held her. "Rosie found all of the items that Clarissa pulled out of your box and stored them safely away," he whispered into her hair.

She tried to pull back, but he held her. "My box?" she asked.

"Yeah, Clarissa told me what she did," he said. "But nothing was destroyed. It's still safe."

A tear ran down her cheek and she brushed it away. "Thank you," she said. "It's just stuff, but…"

"It's important stuff," he said, kissing her head. "I love you, Mary."

Yawning widely, her day catching up with her, she burrowed against him, content and drowsy. "I love you too," she said.

Chapter Two

The room was dark and Mary was trying to understand why she was there. She moved forward tentatively, trying to find an exit door or a light. She didn't feel afraid, but she knew she didn't really belong there. A low sound, like the thrum of a bass note, was pulsing in the background, over some hidden speaker system. Everywhere she went, the sound was present. She continued forward and heard another sound, soft and whispered, in the distance. The sound of a child's cry. Dismissing caution, she hurried forward toward the source of the sound. Running down dark corridors that turned and twisted, she became even more frustrated. Finding herself at a dead end, she turned back and found a staircase that hadn't been there before. She jogged up stairs and down stairs, still following the elusive cry. Finally, she arrived at a door at the far end of a narrow hall. Light flooded out from beneath the door and around the sides into the dark hallway. The door was small and she had to kneel down to grasp the doorknob. The crying became louder, the baby was in distress. Mary yanked on the door, but it wouldn't open. She braced her feet on either side of the door and pulled on the knob, but it was stuck fast. "Help me," she cried out. "Help me save the baby."

"Mary. Mary, wake up," Bradley said softly.

"What? What's wrong?" she asked wearily, trying to fully wake up.

"You were having a bad dream," he said. "You were calling out in your sleep and you were thrashing around like something was attacking you."

The baby! she thought. *I was dreaming about a baby.*

"Did I say anything?" she asked.

"Yeah, but it wasn't in a language I understood," he replied with a crooked smile. "Something like 'oooo-ooo' and 'ahhhh-ahhhh.' I thought you might be conversing with chimpanzees."

"Funny," she said, rolling towards him and resting her hand on his shoulder. "Sorry I woke you up."

"Hey, that's okay," he said, wrapping his arms around her. He leaned over and placed a kiss on her forehead. "I was actually just sitting here, watching you sleep."

She yawned and cuddled closer. "Watching me sleep?" she asked. "Well, that's exciting and a little creepy."

Chuckling softly, he laid his cheek on her head. "Well, it's about as exciting as I want for now."

"Is everything okay?" she asked.

14

Nodding, he leaned back in his pillow. "Right now, things are great. But I was just thinking about how many times I've nearly lost you in the past year," he said. "And all of the other things we've gone through. No wonder we're stressed."

"Who's stressed?" she asked. "I'm not stressed."

"No, nightmares with chimpanzees chasing you are normal."

"Well, maybe I've been watching the National Geographic channel," she countered. "It could be that simple."

"Mary, the first year of marriage is hard enough," he said. "Two people adjusting to living life together, that's stress enough. Then when you add in all the other things in our lives."

"But, those things are part of our lives, our jobs," she said. "It's just who we are."

He tightened his arms around her. "I just don't want any more bad things to happen to you."

Turning, she placed a kiss on his bare chest. "Well, some of the things were good things, right?"

She ran her hand seductively across his chest. "Right?" she repeated.

He gently stroked her back in return. "Um, hmm," he whispered, feeling the heat grow. "Very good things."

Trying to keep the mood light, because of her injuries, he kissed her lightly on the top of her head again. "I just want to make sure we don't add stress to our lives. Don't get ourselves worked up over nothing."

Biting back a smile, she leaned over and kissed him again. "I'm already worked up."

He looked down at her. "How are you feeling?" he asked. "Physically?"

Grinning with eyes sparkling, she teased. "You tell me."

With a sigh of relief, he ran his hands slowly up the sides of her body. "I think you feel good, really good."

"Mmmmm," she purred. "I think I feel great."

He rolled to his side, so he was leaning over her, then bent over and started nuzzling her neck. "Let's see if we can't upgrade great to amazing," he murmured.

She felt the heat growing in her body and wrapped her arms around his neck. "Okay," she moaned softly. "And afterward, we can talk about…"

she gasped when he stroked her body. "…about stress."

"Sure," he mumbled, moving his lips to cover hers and ending any and all coherent thought.

Much later, Mary lay in his arms, exhausted, but relaxed. "So, do you want to talk?" she asked, hiding a yawn.

He pulled her into his arms and shook his head. "No, all I want to do is sleep," he said.

"So, you're not worried now," she murmured, fighting to keep her eyes open.

He kissed the top of her head and snuggled into the blankets. "Tell you what," he said slowly as sleep started to sweep over him. "As long as we keep things status quo for a little while I'm good. Just no surprises, that shouldn't be too hard. Right?"

Eyes suddenly wide open; Mary stared at the snoozing Bradley with dismay. "Right. Not too hard at all," she said aloud, yet silently she thought, *Well, crap!*

Chapter Three

"Good morning ladies," Bradley said, as he entered the kitchen, still adjusting his tie, on Monday morning. "How is everyone today?"

"I'm not a lady, but I'm just fine, thanks for asking," Mike said, gliding over to Bradley.

"I'm good, Daddy," Clarissa replied with a giggle, as she crunched on a piece of toast. "I helped Mary, I mean, Mom, make breakfast."

Standing next to the kitchen counter, putting Clarissa's lunch together, Mary stopped what she was doing for a moment. "Clarissa," she said, keeping her voice matter-of-fact. "It's okay for you to call me Mary. I want you to do what makes you feel comfortable, not what you think you ought to do."

Placing her toast on her plate, Clarissa turned and looked across the kitchen. "You're not mad?" she asked.

"Mary has never been mad at you, Clarissa," Bradley said, sitting down at the table next to his daughter.

Shaking her head, Mary came around the counter and walked over to the table, sitting down on the other side of the little girl. She met her eyes and shook her head. "I'm not mad at all," she said. "What you call me doesn't matter. I just want to be sure that we are honest with each other. Honest about our feelings and that we try to work together as a family."

"We all have to do that," Bradley said. "We all need to be sure we are talking to each other and telling the truth."

"You don't hate me?" Clarissa asked Mary. "For what I did to you?"

"Hey, Clarissa, Mary doesn't work that way," Mike said. "She'll tell you the truth."

Leaning over and placing a soft kiss on the child's forehead, Mary said, "No, I love you. And not because you are Bradley's daughter, but because you are you."

"Really?" she asked, turning to Mike, skepticism evident in her eyes.

"Angel's honor," Mike said, crossing his finger over his heart.

She turned and looked at Mary. "Really?" she asked again.

Mary nodded. "Yes, really," she said. "But you don't have to take my word on it. Watch me and let me prove it."

"I think that's fair," Bradley added.

Clarissa sat quietly for a moment and then asked, "So does that mean you're going to let me do anything I want to do?"

Mike laughed out loud. "Working all the angles, aren't you?"

Chuckling, Mary placed her hand on Clarissa's head and tousled her hair. "Not a chance," she said. "Loving someone doesn't mean they give you everything."

Sighing, Clarissa nodded. "Yeah, that's what Mrs. Brennan says too."

"Well, if Mrs. Brennan agrees, then I must be doing something right," she said. "But I know we still have a lot of things to work out, so I'm going to call a friend of mine and see what we should be doing to help us become a better family."

"Okay," Clarissa agreed. "That sounds like a good idea."

"Yes, it does," Bradley said. "We all need to help, including me."

"Good!" Mary replied, standing up quickly. She grabbed the table as a sudden rush of dizziness hit her. The room started to tilt and she felt lightheaded.

Bradley jumped to his feet and was immediately at her side. "Mary?" he asked. "What's wrong?"

Mike glided over to the other side of her. "Hey, champ, take it easy."

Taking a deep breath, she lowered herself slowly back into the chair. "I just think I stood up too fast," she said. "I just got a little dizzy, that's all."

"I'm taking you to the hospital," Bradley said.

"Yeah, because that's her favorite place in the whole wide world," Mike murmured.

Chuckling, Mary shook her head. "No, really, I'm fine," she replied. "Because of the medication, I've been off of caffeine for a couple of days; I'm sure that's it. Just a little light-leaded, that's all."

Bradley was not mollified. "Have you eaten anything?" he asked, as he poured a glass of milk and placed it before her.

"She hasn't," Clarissa chimed in. "She's been busy doing other stuff."

Bradley turned to his daughter. "I think it's time we do some stuff for Mary," he said. "What do you think?"

She smiled. "I think it's a great idea," she agreed.

"Okay, Mary, what would you like for breakfast?" Bradley asked.

Sweet and sour chicken, Mary thought and then said, "Toast with strawberry preserves."

"I can make that," Clarissa exclaimed, hopping out of her chair and dashing to the toaster.

Bradley sat down next to Mary. "Okay, tell me how you really feel," he said softly.

"Kind of silly," Mary admitted. "But, fine, really. I just need to take things a little slower right now."

"Yes, your body needs time to adjust," he replied.

"Adjust?" she repeated. Did he know about the baby?

"Yes, you need to adjust to being back on your feet after being in bed all weekend."

Nodding slowly, she exhaled softly. "Yes, you're right," she agreed. "That's probably it."

"Can I get you a Diet Pepsi?" he asked.

Shaking her head sadly, she said, "No, since I've been off caffeine all weekend and I survived, this is probably a good time to start cutting back. But I'd love some herb tea."

"You've got it," he said.

Mary turned and watched Bradley and Clarissa hurry around the kitchen, making breakfast for her and a lump formed in her throat.

"So, what is it you're not telling us?" Mike whispered.

She smiled up at him and shook her head. "I'm good," she replied.

He looked at her, and then looked across the room. Bradley was instructing Clarissa on how to put only a little butter on the toast, while he helped remove the thick coating she had already put on it. "You're all going to make it," he said softly.

She smiled up at him, absently placed her hand on her stomach and nodded. *This is going to work*, she decided adamantly. *We are going to make a great family.*

Chapter Four

After assuring Bradley that she could drive her car, Mary finally arrived at her office a little after nine o'clock and Rosie was already waiting for her at the front door.

"Well, you're here bright and early," Mary said, as she stepped out of her car, pulling her purse and computer bag along with her. "How was your Sunday?"

"Stanley and I had a nice quiet Sunday, just being lazy," she replied, as she studied Mary's face. "But more importantly, how are you feeling?"

Trying to smile convincingly, she nodded. "I'm good. Much better. Thanks so much for all you did on Saturday."

"All I did was to nearly get you and Clarissa killed because I didn't watch her," Rosie said, her eyes downcast. "I can't tell you how sorry I—"

"Rosie, it wasn't your fault," Mary insisted as she put her arm around her friend. "Clarissa wasn't honest with you. You thought she was safe and secure with Katie. You would have never left her otherwise."

"But—" she began.

"No buts," Mary replied. "It simply was not your fault. Okay?"

Rosie nodded. "Okay," she exhaled softly.

Unlocking the door to her office, she held it open for Rosie and then put her things on the desk. "Have a seat," she offered. "I'm just going to start my computer."

She pulled her laptop out of the bag and attached it to the docking station on her desk. She powered on the laptop and then sat down in her chair and turned to Rosie. "So, what's up?" she asked.

"Actually, I'm here with a business proposal," she said and lifting one eyebrow added, "A paying business proposal."

"Well, this is a great way to start a Monday morning," Mary replied with a smile. "What can I do for you?"

Searching through her purse for a moment, Rosie finally pulled out an index card and handed it to Mary. "This is a listing of mine," she said. "A lovely old home out in the country. The house is large and well-maintained and the acreage around it is breathtaking, but we've been trying to sell it for over a year and there are no bites."

Mary looked at the address. It was on a quiet road between Freeport and Lena, a nice area. "Is it overpriced?" she asked.

Shaking her head, Rosie scooted forward in her seat and lowered her voice. "It's haunted."

"Actively haunted, like ghosts showing up during an Open House?" Mary asked.

"No, nothing like that," Rosie said. "Just an uncomfortable feeling when you enter the house. Everyone who's taken a tour loves the outside, but once they are inside, they want to hurry out. No one knows why. Or at least, they aren't willing to say why."

"Did anyone die in the house?" Mary asked.

Rosie nodded slowly. "Yes, although the owners didn't talk about it, I did some research," she explained. "The husband of the woman who is selling died in a farming accident. He was suffocated in a grain silo. I think he's haunting the house."

"Well, that would make sense," Mary said. "Perhaps he doesn't know he's dead."

"That's what I thought too," Rosie agreed with a smile. "I thought you could just come out to the house and have a conversation with him and then he could move on."

Sitting back in her chair, Mary folded her arms over her chest. "You know it's not always that easy," she said. "What does your client think about having me check things out?"

Avoiding Mary's eyes, Rosie chewed her lower lip nervously. "Well, about that," she began.

"You didn't tell her," Mary supplied.

"No, I didn't," she confessed. "But she's not your client. The brokerage is your client. If we can sell this place, we're going to earn a tidy commission."

"But if she finds out—" Mary began.

"Our contract states that we can call in a specialist if we feel it will help us sell the properties," she interrupted. "At our expense, of course. So, why would she care?"

"Oh, I don't know," Mary said with a smile. "Perhaps there are skeletons in their closets."

Rosie smiled back. "Then we should be sure you have a look at all of the closets too," she replied. "When can you go?"

Mary chuckled, of course she was going and Rosie knew it. "I have a couple of calls to make. They might take a while," she said. "Can I call you when I'm done?"

"That would be perfect," Rosie said, standing and smiling down at Mary. "You make your calls and then we'll take a nice drive in the country."

"That sounds lovely," Mary said. "I'll call you as soon as I'm free."

Chapter Five

"District 43, Gracie Williams speaking. What can I do for you?" the familiar voice answered.

Mary smiled just thinking of her friend. "Hi, Gracie, this is Mary O'Reilly," she said.

"You mean Mary Alden, don't you?" Gracie asked. "Unless that man of yours has done something stupid and you are already kicking his butt out of the house."

"Oh, no, nothing like that," she said with a laugh. "We decided that I should keep using my maiden name for my business and I guess I don't have a lot of practice saying Mary Alden yet."

"Yeah, it might be a little complicated in your business to have the same name as the Chief of Police," she replied. "So what can I do for you?"

"I need some professional advice," Mary admitted.

"You still seeing ghosts?" Gracie asked.

"Yes," Mary answered.

"Honey, I can't help you there," she said. "We both know you got something going on there beyond my professional ability to figure out."

"No, it's not that," Mary said. "It's Clarissa."

"Clarissa, Bradley's daughter?" Gracie asked.

"Yes, she's been acting out a little lately," Mary said. "And I'm not sure what to do."

"When you say acting out, what exactly do you mean?" Gracie asked.

"Do you have a few minutes?" Mary asked.

"Excuse me for a moment, sweetie," Gracie replied.

Mary could hear some movement, like Gracie was getting out of her chair and then heard footsteps across a wood floor. Then she heard Gracie's voice in the distance. "Claire, I need you to hold my calls and visitors for the next hour. And reschedule that ten o'clock meeting," she said. "I've got an important phone conference."

A moment later, Gracie was back. "Okay, sugar, why don't you just tell Gracie all about it."

Forty-five minutes later Mary was reaching for another tissue, wiping her eyes and finishing her explanation to Gracie. She took a deep, shuddering breath and said, "And that's about it. So, what have I done wrong?"

"Well, sugar, the only thing you've done wrong is blame yourself," Gracie replied. "That little girl has gone through an awful lot of hurt in her young life. She has had no stability, no safety, and no structure for a very long time. And she was kind of used to running the show. She took care of everyone else, that's what made her feel important. That's what she thought her value was. Now you walk in, take care of her and Bradley, and she's feeling insecure. She doesn't know where she fits and she doesn't want to get used to loving you in case you both change your mind and up and die on her."

"We're not going to die," Mary said.

"Why not, everyone else has?" Gracie countered. "Look at it from her point of view. Even the bad man died. Anyone who ever wanted her has gone away, why should she trust you and Bradley?"

Mary exhaled slowly. "Okay, I never thought of it that way," she said.

"Course you haven't," Gracie said with a laugh. "That's my job. I don't talk to ghosts and you don't figure out what's inside people's heads, okay?"

"Okay," Mary replied, feeling a little better. "So, what do we do?"

"You get this little girl some help," Gracie said. "Is there a child psychologist you know and trust?"

"I heard of one woman," Mary said, thinking aloud. "Karen Springler. She's supposed to be great with kids, really warm and fuzzy."

"Sounds like the perfect person for the job," Gracie said. "But, if for some reason Clarissa doesn't like her, don't be afraid to find someone she clicks with."

"Should I be attending the sessions too?" Mary asked.

"Well, I'm going to let Dr. Springler run her program the way she likes," Gracie said. "But usually there will be sessions for the whole family and then sessions just for Clarissa."

"Thank you, Gracie," Mary said. "I feel so much better."

"Sure you do, honey," Gracie replied. "Now, why don't you tell me the other thing that's on your mind?"

Surprised, Mary stuttered for a moment. "There's…there's…nothing, really."

"U-huh, you never were a good liar, Mary O'Reilly," Gracie said. "I can tell your lying clear from Chicago."

"I think I'm pregnant," Mary whispered into the phone, glancing at the door to be sure no one was close by.

"Well, halleluiah," Gracie said. "That's wonderful."

"Well, it could be," Mary said.

31

"Honey, it's a damn near miracle if you're pregnant," Gracie said. "And I know you've wanted a baby of your own. So, what's the problem?"

Mary felt the tears welling in her eyes and grabbed for another tissue. "It's Bradley," she said.

"What? I can't believe he doesn't want a baby," Gracie exclaimed.

"No. I mean I don't know," she said. "I haven't told him."

"What?" Gracie roared. "You haven't told him? Why the hell not?"

"Well, you know, with Clarissa and work and all that's going on…" Mary began.

"Oh, no, you are not going to tell me that you think it's your job to protect your husband," Gracie said. "Honey, when are you going to remember it's not your job to always sacrifice yourself for others? Sometimes the people that love you want to be able to sacrifice for you."

"But—" Mary started.

"No," Gracie interrupted. "No, there are no buts here. You call that man, as soon as we hang up this phone. You call him and you get him down to your office and you tell him. You understand?"

"I'm—" Mary said.

32

"Do you understand?" Gracie interrupted once again.

"But what if he's not happy about it?" Mary said, her voice breaking.

"Then he's an idiot. And your man is not an idiot."

"No, he's not," Mary agreed.

"And just because it's in your body, doesn't mean it's not his baby too," she added. "Why keep him from the joy?"

"Shouldn't I wait until I've gone to the doctor, just to be sure?"

"Are you sure?" Gracie asked her.

"Well, I'm…"

"Are you sure?" Gracie repeated. "In your heart."

Mary nodded. "Yes, I'm sure," she said, her smile widening as tears slipped from her eyes. "I'm sure."

"If that baby's a girl, you know her name has to be Gracie," Gracie added with a chuckle. "And if it's a boy, Grayson will be just fine."

"I'll remember that," Mary said with a watery laugh. "Thank you Gracie."

"Don't thank me," she said. "Just call that husband of yours. Goodbye Mary Alden."

"Goodbye Gracie," Mary said, and she hung up the phone.

A moment later she picked it up again and pressed a speed dial number. "Hi Dorothy, it's Mary," she said. "Could I speak with Bradley?"

Chapter Six

Bradley rushed out of his office, pulling on his jacket, as he passed Dorothy's desk. "I'm heading over to Mary's," he said.

"Is she okay?" Dorothy asked.

He nodded slowly. "Yeah, I think so," he replied hesitantly. "I mean, I'm sure... She just wants to talk..."

He froze and stared at Dorothy. "She just wants to talk," he repeated. "That's never good."

"Don't worry about it, Chief," Dorothy said with what she hoped was an encouraging smile. "Everything's fine."

Bradley looked at the grimace pasted on Dorothy's face and his stomach dropped. He'd better hurry. "Thanks, Dorothy," he said, trying to hide his alarm. "I'll call you if I'm going to be a while."

Rather than take his cruiser and try and find parking, Bradley decided to jog the three short blocks to Mary's office. Maybe the run in the cool spring air would help his sense of dread. The lights worked in his favor and he jogged across Galena Avenue, turning right toward Main Street.

What could be wrong? he asked himself. *Mary was great this morning at breakfast. Last night was...*he smiled as he remembered their night together. *...amazing. If it had been an emergency, she would have told me. Or would she? What if the hospital called? What if they found something?*

He broke into a run for the final block and threw the door open to Mary's office. "What's wrong?" he panted, putting his hands on his knees while he caught his breath.

"Hi," she said nervously, avoiding eye contact with him. "Why don't you, um, have a seat."

Something is wrong. Something is very wrong, Bradley thought as he slipped into the chair across from her. "What's up?" he asked, trying to sound casual.

"I… I had a great conversation with Gracie this morning," she said quickly. "She suggests we bring Clarissa to a child psychologist so she can talk about everything that's happened to her. She thinks that will really help Clarissa."

Bradley nodded. "Well, good, that sounds like a great idea," he said. "Do you have someone in mind?"

"Yes, I do," Mary replied. "Actually, I already called her and she can meet with all of us tomorrow afternoon, if that works for you."

Bradley sat back in the chair and ran his hand through his hair. "That works for me," he answered quickly. "But Mary, is that why you asked me to come to your office?"

"No," she confessed, shaking her head quickly. "No it's not. I'm just stalling."

Quickly sitting up and moving to the edge of his seat, Bradley leaned forward over the desk and took Mary's hands in his own. "What is it?" he asked. "You can tell me anything."

Taking a deep breath, she shook her head. "The other night, Saturday night, when the hospital called, the nurse mentioned something…" she began.

Bradley jumped up from the chair, came around the desk and knelt down next to her. "Mary, what's wrong?" he asked. "I had a feeling there was something you weren't telling me. But whatever it is, we can work through it."

She nodded, her eyes filling with tears. "Well, it was just so unexpected," she said. "And I knew we were going through all kinds of stress and I didn't want to add one more thing to the list."

Bradley froze, staring at her for a moment. "How bad is it?" he asked. "How long do you have?"

Talking over him, she continued to explain. "And really I never even thought it was possible, given the surgery," she continued. "So I didn't take precautions, because really, why bother?"

"It's related to the shooting?" he asked. "Did something happen to your organs? Weaken you? Damage something and now they're finding it?"

"And then, everything is going to change in nine months," she said, not hearing him and wiping away her tears. "I mean we just started our new family, nine months is not a lot of time to have together before things change."

Bradley stood up, clapping his hand over his mouth, his stomach dropping to his feet. "Nine months," he finally said, shaking his head in disbelief. "You only have nine months. I don't know what to say."

He paced away from her, trying to get his emotions under control. He was going to lose Mary in nine months. How would he ever continue on?

He heard her chair push away from the desk and she came up behind him, lacing her arms around his waist and placing her head on his back. "I'm sorry, Bradley. I should have—"

"No," he interrupted, his voice hoarse. "Don't blame yourself. I don't want our last nine months to be wasted in blame."

"Our last nine months?" she exclaimed tearfully. "You're going to leave me?"

He slowly turned and looked down at her. "What are we talking about?"

"I guess you're leaving me in nine months," she replied, tears rolling down her cheeks and her voice shaking.

"I thought you were leaving me in nine months," he said.

Wiping tears off her face with the back of her hand, she shook her head angrily. "How could I leave you in nine months?" she asked. "The baby will be brand new."

Bradley gasped, like he had been punched in the solar plexus. "The baby?" he asked.

"Yes, the baby," she replied. "I'm pregnant. What do you think I've been trying to tell you?"

Having been emotionally transported from abject misery to utter amazement, for a moment all Bradley could do was stare at Mary, his mouth hanging open.

Swallowing nervously, Mary waited for a moment before asking. "Do you really hate the idea?"

Slowly, not saying a word, he knelt before her, wrapped his arms around her waist and laid his head against her abdomen. Then he turned his head and kissed her stomach. She enfolded his head in her arms and held him there, tears of joy slipping down her cheeks.

"Our baby," he whispered. "I can't believe it."

"Are you happy about it?" she asked.

He turned his head up and looked at her. She saw the wonder through the tears.

"Happy?" he replied. "Happy doesn't begin to describe what I'm feeling. I'm overwhelmed."

She bent over and placed a kiss on his forehead. "I love you," she said.

He stood and swept her into his arms. "I love you," he said, crushing her lips with his own.

Finally, a few moments later, he lifted his head and smiled tenderly down at her. "We're having a baby."

Eyes glowing with love, she nodded. "Yeah, looks like it," she agreed. "I'm going to see the doctor this afternoon."

"Okay, I'll be there," he replied.

"Will you?" she asked, overjoyed.

He kissed her again. "Of course I will," he answered after a moment. "This is our baby."

Walking across the room to her desk, he carefully placed her in the chair. "So, can I get you anything?" he asked. "Something to eat?"

She smiled up at him. "No, I'm great. I'm perfect," she said with a deep sigh of relief. "I'm so happy you reacted this way. I thought the news would be just another added stress."

He leaned over and kissed her again. "A baby is a blessing, not a stress," he said. "So, when shall we tell Clarissa?"

Mary sat back in her chair and placed her hand protectively on her abdomen. "Well, there is something else you should know," she said. "The hospital said the positive test indicated that I was pregnant, but after what happened to me on Saturday, that could be changed."

Kneeling in front of her chair, Bradley placed his hand over hers. "You mean you might not be pregnant anymore?"

She nodded. "I thought about waiting until after my appointment to tell you," she admitted. "Just so…"

"So you could save me from the disappointment," he added. "Mary, you do remember the whole 'for better and for worse' part of the ceremony right?"

She shrugged and looked away. "Yes, but…"

41

Lifting his other hand, he gently cupped her cheek and turned her towards him. "I'm glad you told me, not only because I will be able to be there for you when you get the news, good or bad. But also because it lets us both know you can get pregnant. So, if for some reason this baby isn't meant to be, we know there'll be others."

He tenderly rubbed his thumb across her cheek, catching the single tear that made its way down her face. "We're a team, right," he said softly, with a crooked smile. "Go team."

She chuckled quietly. "Yeah, go team," she replied and then sniffed back the tears. "But as far as Clarissa, I think we should wait until we know for sure. She doesn't need any more sadness right now."

Nodding, he stood and kissed her again. "You're absolutely right," he said. "Let's see what the doctor says and then we can decide on what's best to tell her. Okay?"

"Okay," Mary replied. "Now, you should go back to keeping Freeport safe for all its residents and I'll get to work."

He stayed where he was, bent over her chair. "You'll take it easy? Promise?" he asked.

Grinning, she nodded. "I promise," she said. "And thanks for worrying."

"Oh, don't thank me," he said with a returning smile. "I promise I'm going to be a pain in the butt about watching over you. Just warning you."

"Okay, just occasionally remind me that I did thank you," she replied. "Once."

Suddenly serious, he bent once more and kissed her tenderly. "I thought I could never love you more than I did when I asked you to marry me," he whispered softly. "I was wrong."

Chapter Seven

"Thanks for doing this for me," Rosie said, as she drove down Highway 20 away from Freeport. "I really think this house needs a family, but something is pushing everyone away."

Mary sat back in the comfortable leather seat of Rosie's SUV and nodded. "No problem," she said. "I just need to be back in my office by three because I have a three thirty doctor's appointment."

Rosie glanced over at Mary, then back to the road. "Is it a follow-up visit from what happened on Saturday?" she asked, concerned. "Maybe you shouldn't be doing this, Mary. You should be home, resting. I can't believe I asked you to do this. I'm turning around right now."

Mary placed her hand softly on Rosie's arm. "I'm fine, Rosie," she assured her. "It's not a follow-up visit. It's something completely different."

Rosie turned to protest but stopped when she noticed the peaceful smile on Mary's face. *What in the world?*

"Are you sure you're fine?" she asked. "I still feel bad about what happened—"

"Rosie," Mary interrupted. "I think I'm pregnant."

"What?" Rosie exclaimed, gasping in delight. "Are you sure?"

"We're going to the doctor this afternoon," she explained. "The hospital did a routine check that turned out positive, but I don't think we're really going to know until they can hear a heartbeat."

"How long does that take?" Rosie asked.

"Not for at least a couple more weeks," Mary replied. "But, since I haven't shown any signs of losing the baby, I'm going to believe I'm still pregnant."

"Mary, that is just so wonderful," Rosie said. "I'm sure Bradley and Clarissa are thrilled."

"Well, Bradley's thrilled," Mary said. "But we haven't told Clarissa yet. We want to make sure everything's okay before we tell her. She doesn't need any more loss in her life."

"Why, I suppose that's a good idea," Rosie said. "Until you know for sure."

Rosie turned right from Highway 20 onto a smaller road. "We're almost to the little farm," she said. "Are you sure you're feeling up to this?"

"I feel great," Mary said.

"Okay, well, then let's find out what secrets this house is hiding," she replied as she pulled the

45

SUV into the gravel driveway and in front of the house.

Mary stepped out of the SUV and stared at the house. It was a large wood-framed home, with a graceful wraparound porch, a picture window in the front and a porch swing just waiting for an occupant. Rosie was right, it needed a family. It was a place for family gatherings. She could picture a Christmas tree in the front window, with the porch strewn with lights and garland or friends and families gathering for a country Thanksgiving, arms filled with dishes as they walked up the stairs, greeted by loved ones. This house had great memories, but it needed more.

"I see what you mean," Mary said to Rosie, over the hood of the vehicle. "Let's go in."

They walked up the steps and Rosie unlocked the door, leading the way into the house.

The front hallway had a staircase to the left and a doorway ahead of them. Mary paused, waiting to see if she felt a prompting to go upstairs or continue through the first floor. She had a little twist in her stomach as she looked through the doorway that led to the dining room. "Let's go this way," she suggested, walking down the hallway.

The old wood floors glistened in the sunlight that poured through the lace-curtained windows. The house was chilly, but it seemed to Mary to be more the cause of a low thermostat setting than anything supernatural. She walked through the dining room, into a great room with a wood stove on a red brick hearth. *This would be cozy*, she thought.

Walking slowly around the empty room, Mary could sense a feeling of family in the room. She could see shadows of the families who had lived here; children standing around the wood stove in the early morning hours enjoying the warmth as they talked and laughed, other children playing board games on a coffee table, a child laying on a couch covered with a quilt as a worried mother hovered nearby and hushed voices and the patter of little feet as they rushed down the stairs to greet the magic of Christmas. There was nothing scary or supernatural here, just memories, good memories, of growing up. There had to be something else wrong with the house, because it really didn't seem to be haunted. Turning to Rosie, she was about to suggest they leave when she saw a movement in the kitchen.

Hurrying across the room, she walked through the doorway to the big country kitchen.

"What are you doing in my house?" the man demanded.

Mary turned and gasped. He was standing in the far corner of the kitchen, near the back door. He was wearing an old barn jacket over a pair of worn overalls. But his head was twisted sideways and it was too narrow and long, as if it had been crushed.

She looked carefully and saw his body also seemed to have been broken by the way he stood.

"I'm not going to ask you again," he snapped. "What are you doing in my house?"

"Hi, I'm Mary," she said, approaching him. "Mary O'Reilly. I was invited here because your family is interested in selling the house."

"What the hell?" he growled. "We're not selling this place. This place has been in our family for generations. I don't give a damn what those land speculators say, we ain't selling, not one acre."

"Well, I agree with you, Mr—" Mary paused.

"Johnson. Dale Johnson," he replied, gliding over to her. "I own this place. Don't do all the running of it anymore - my kids do that- but I still own every single square foot."

"It's a beautiful place," Mary agreed. "I don't blame you for not wanting to sell it."

He smiled and nodded. "Yes, it is beautiful and it's got plenty of good memories wrapped up inside it. And I thank you for being so polite. I've had my house invaded for the last little while by strangers who think they can just walk all over without even a 'how do you do.' I follow them around the house, demanding they leave, but they just ignore me. Peeking in my closets and opening my drawers, who the hell do they think they are?"

"This might seem like an odd question," Mary said. "But what's the last thing you remember doing on your farm?"

He paused for a moment, walked over to the back door and stared outside. "Why, I fed the calves," he said slowly, "Just like I do every night. Had Buster, my dog, with me. I remember it was getting a might chilly and I could tell winter wasn't too far off."

"Then what did you do?" Mary asked.

"I watered the calves and then…," he stopped and then turned to her. "The door to the grain silo was open. Sometimes those boys are just careless. Full grown men and they can't even remember to latch the silo door. I need to remember to talk to them about that."

"So, did you latch the door?"

"Well, let me see now," he said, scratching the side of his misshapen head. "I remember going into the silo, just to be sure no one was in there. You don't want to be caught in a locked silo during the harvest."

"That makes sense," Mary said. "Was anyone in there?"

"No. It was all cleaned out, ready for the corn," he said. "The boys were out in the field with the combines and the trucks, trying to get the grain in

49

before we got rain. They were working like crazy 'cause they waited until the last minute again. I told them they could have pulled that grain in a week earlier, but no, they wanted a couple more days of drying. Don't know what good that did anyhow."

"Do you remember latching the door?" Mary asked. "Or talking with your sons?"

"I...I remember looking around the inside of the silo," he said slowly. "And then... And then I remember hitting my head. Can't imagine what I'd hit my head on, but it knocked me off my feet and onto the ground. I woke up a little while later and..."

He stopped, turned back to the door and looked out the window. Mary could see he was still running the event through his mind.

"What the hell?" he said softly and then turned and met Mary's eyes. "I don't remember getting out of the silo. I don't remember anything..."

Eyes widening, he shook his head. "I didn't leave, did I?"

"No," Mary said. "You didn't leave. You got trapped in there and died."

"I died?" he asked, his voice hoarse and unsure. "I'm dead?"

He glided past her, rushing into the dining room. "Greta! Greta, where are you?"

Mary turned to Rosie who had been standing back next to the doorway to the great room. "Who is Greta?" she asked.

"Greta is, well, was, his wife," Rosie said. "They moved her to an assisted living home because her kids didn't think it was safe for her to be living out here all by herself."

"All by herself?" Mary asked. "Didn't the kids live close by because of the farm?"

"Oh, no, most of the farm property was sold off years ago," Rosie said. "All they had left was the house and these five acres."

"Well Dale is not going to be happy about that," Mary said.

Chapter Eight

Mary climbed the stairs to the second floor and found Dale sitting in the middle of the master bedroom sobbing. He looked up when Mary entered the room.

"Is my Greta dead too?" he asked.

Mary sat down on the wood floor next to him. "No, she's still alive. She's older now and needed a little more help, so she's living in an assisted living home."

"How's she doing?" he asked.

"I don't know," she replied. "I haven't met her yet. But I would be happy to go to her and bring her a message from you."

He didn't answer, just looked around the room. "So, is this hell?" he asked. "Being stuck in a place that holds all your memories, but you sit here without the people you love?"

"It probably seems like hell," Mary agreed. "But, no, actually you're still on earth."

"I'm dead, but I'm still on earth. What am I, a ghost?" he scoffed.

"For lack of a better word, yes, that's exactly what you are."

He rose to his feet and stared down at her, affronted. "I don't believe in ghosts, young lady," he said. "And I was a good Christian man. If I died, I should have been sent to heaven."

Mary suddenly felt nauseous and took a deep shaky breath.

Dale stopped his tirade and knelt down next to her. "Are you okay?" he asked. "You looked a bit peaked."

She nodded slowly. "I think it has something to do with being pregnant," she said. "I just found out."

He smiled kindly. "This your first?" he asked.

"Yes," she said, stroking her stomach. "I'm a real novice."

"Well, my Greta got sick as a dog for the first three months," he said. "And after that, it was smooth sailing."

"What did she do for the sickness?" Mary asked.

"Seems to me, she always carried soda crackers around with her, everywhere she went," he said.

Mary felt her stomach twisting. "And if she didn't have soda crackers?"

"She made a beeline to the toilet and didn't hold back," he replied. "Said she always felt better once she got it out of her system."

Mary took another deep breath. "Bathroom?" she asked.

Dale moved out of the way and pointed. "Last door on the left at the end of the hall."

He was right, Mary thought a few minutes later as she splashed cold water on her face over the bathroom sink. *I do feel better.*

She pulled a tissue out of her coat pocket, blotted her face, opened the bathroom door and met a concerned Rosie in the hallway. "Are you okay?" Rosie said. "I thought I heard…"

"Morning sickness," Mary supplied. "Yeah, I feel much better now. Thanks."

"I have some crackers in my purse," Rosie volunteered. "It's in the car, but I'll only be a moment."

Thinking that crackers actually sounded good, Mary nodded. "Thanks, that would be nice. I'll be in the master bedroom talking with Dale."

Looking down the hall, she could see Dale standing in the doorway watching her. "I'm feeling much better," she admitted, as she got closer. "Thanks for the advice."

Chuckling, he moved away from the door as she entered. "Always worked for Greta," he said. "Every morning, like clockwork, she'd dash down the hall to the bathroom. Got to give her credit for doing it three times. I wouldn't have lasted through one."

He glided to the window and looked down at Rosie opening her car door. "So, can your friend see me too?" he asked.

Shaking her head, Mary followed him to the window. "No, she can't. But she could feel your presence. That's why she asked me to come by."

"You're an expert?"

Laughing, she shrugged. "Well, I guess you could call me that," she said. "I've been doing this for a couple of years."

"What do you mean by doing this?"

"I find people who have died, ghosts, and help them figure out why they're still here," she said. "So they can continue on to heaven."

He turned to her. "What's holding me back?"

"I don't know," she answered. "What do you think it is?"

He glided away from her to a side window that overlooked the old grain silo. Vines and brush had grown up around it and the barn had fallen into a state of disrepair. The pens that had housed the calves were now gone; only broken slabs of concrete with grass growing up between them remained.

"What happened to my farm?" he asked.

"Rosie, my friend, told me that all of it was sold off," Mary explained, "except for the house and five acres. Your wife lived here since your death."

"But, we talked about selling it off," he said, shaking his head in confusion. "We all decided that we needed to keep it. We didn't want some big corporate farm to get the land."

"You all decided?" Mary asked.

"Yeah, well, Josh, my oldest son wanted to sell the farm," Dale said. "He said we could get enough money for all of us to do whatever we wanted to do. I told him I wanted to farm. Told him that if farming was good enough for his grandfather and his great-grandfather, it ought to be good enough for him."

"What did the other children think?" Mary asked.

"Abe, my youngest boy, was a farmer, just like me," he said. "He wanted to hold on to the land."

"And your daughter?"

"Jessie was siding with Josh," he said. "She wanted to move away from Freeport. She wanted to live in the big city. She even had a boyfriend from Chicago."

"So you voted?" Mary asked.

"Hell no," he replied. "The land was mine. The boys worked it and Jessie did the books. I paid them well. But the land was mine. And no one was going to sell it. Over my dead body."

Mary didn't say a word and watched as Dale realized the meaning of his words. "My dead body," he repeated slowly, turning and looking at Mary. "I got hit in the back of the head. I didn't bump my head. When I woke up, someone had locked the door. I pounded on it and I screamed, but no one opened the door. It was a trap."

He slowly sunk to the floor and laid his head in his hands. "Damn it all to hell," he whispered. "I was murdered."

Chapter Nine

Rosie locked the door and they both started to walk down the porch stairs when a pickup truck pulled into the gravel driveway. They both waited on the porch until the truck stopped and the passenger got out. He was a short and wiry older man with a John Deere cap resting on his head. He looked at the two women and tipped the brim of his hat in their direction.

"Afternoon," he said, walking around the front of the truck and coming to the porch.

"Hello," Rosie replied, taking a protective step in front of Mary. "Can I help you?"

"Well, that's kinda what I wanted to ask you," he replied. "This here house is empty and I know the owners and, quite frankly, you ain't them."

Rosie smiled, pulled a card out of her pocket and handed it to him. "I'm Rosie Wagner," she explained, "a real estate broker. I'm handling the sale of Greta Johnson's home. And this is Mary, she's interested in the home."

"Oh, I see," he said as he studied the card. "I'm afraid I have to apologize, ladies. I'm Greta's neighbor, Sawyer Gartner. I own the property next door. There's been some break-ins out here in the country, especially when folks aren't home during the day. So I always keep my eyes open."

"Yes, actually Jessie mentioned the break-ins which is why we didn't put a For Sale sign out in front of the house, we didn't want to advertise that it was empty," Rosie said. "But it's nice to know they also have a concerned neighbor."

"Well, the Johnson's are good people, always have been," he said. "And that's what farmers do; we look out for each other."

Mary stepped forward. "Have you always lived next door?" she asked.

He nodded. "Yeah, the Johnsons and the Gartners have farmed next to each other for generations. I grew up with Dale."

"I agree with Rosie, it's nice to know there are nice neighbors around," Mary said.

"You won't find a nicer place to raise a family," Sawyer said. "Nothing like room to run."

Mary nodded. "You're right, this place seems ideal."

****

A little while later, the two women were back in Rosie's SUV driving back towards town. "If he really was murdered, then someone in his family is a murderer," Rosie exclaimed, as she turned onto

59

Highway 20. "And they seemed to be such lovely people."

"Just because he believes he was murdered, doesn't necessarily make it true," Mary said. "It still could have been just a farming accident. There still could be another reason. But, in order for him to move on, we need to solve the mystery."

"A murderer," Rosie said. "I signed a house contract with a murderer. Why they could have killed me right there on the spot. Signed the contract and 'poof' just off the real estate broker." She paused for a moment. "They still do say 'off' don't they?"

Rolling her eyes, Mary replied. "Yes, they do still say 'off' but generally only in the movies. And, Rosie, why would they kill you? They want you to sell their house."

Exhaling deeply, Rosie nodded. "That's right," she exclaimed. "I'm not a threat. I'm just an innocent real estate broker."

She turned and grinned at Mary. "Well, maybe not that innocent," she inserted with a snicker. "But I'm not a threat. I don't know anything...Wait, I do know something now. I know they killed their father."

"Rosie, you don't know they killed their father because their father is a ghost and people don't believe in ghosts," Mary said.

"That's right," Rosie agreed, nodding her head purposefully. Then she paused and turned to Mary. "But, really, we do believe in ghosts, right?"

"Yes, *we* do. But *they* don't. So we can't tell them or they will think you're a kook and they will cancel the contract."

"And we can't solve the murder case if we don't have a contract," Rosie added.

"Exactly," Mary said.

"So, should I be carrying when I show the house?" she asked.

"Not unless you're going to be showing it to gangsters," Mary answered.

"Gangsters are interested in the house?" Rosie cried.

Mary couldn't help herself; she threw her head back and laughed. "Oh, Rosie, I just adore you," she said, then after a moment to pull herself together she turned to her friend. "This is how we're going to handle this case. You pretend like nothing is wrong. Continue to show the house and keep the client updated, but don't meet with them in person for now."

Mary knew her dear friend would have a hard time not giving everything away.

"Then, it would be very helpful if you could search back in the real estate records to see how quickly the other parts of the farm were sold off and who bought them," Mary continued. "And if you happen to know the broker who handled the sale, it would be great if we could get copies of the sale."

"I'm sure I can find it," Rosie said. "I'll start looking this afternoon."

"Great," Mary said. "Let's meet tomorrow morning at my office and go through what you've found."

Rosie pulled her car into the parking spot next to her office. "Thank you so much, Mary," she said. "I had no idea it would turn out this way."

Mary leaned over and gave Rosie a hug. "You were right, it's a wonderful home," Mary said. "And it's mostly filled with happy memories. We just need to help Dale move on, and then some lucky family can make it their own."

"You know, you and Bradley should consider it," Rosie said with a smile as she opened her door. "It would be wonderful for a growing family."

"I don't think we need to add buying a new house to our list of things to do," Mary said, joining Rosie on the sidewalk. "I think we have enough on our plates for now."

"Well, if you change your mind," Rosie called as she unlocked her office door.

"Sure, just don't hold your breath," Mary replied with a smile, turning and walking back to her office.

The red button on her answering machine was frantically blinking when she opened the door. She dropped her coat and purse on the chair next to her desk and pressed the messages button.

"Hi Mary, this is Jodi from Union Dairy Ice Cream Parlor," the machine repeated. "I have an…issue here at the store. Something I need your help with. Could you come by today or tomorrow so we could talk?"

Union Dairy Ice Cream Parlor had been a Freeport establishment since the early 1900s when Stephenson County was the dairy farm capitol of Illinois. Recently renovated, the building sported a fifties theme with a bright red linoleum counter, matching red plastic and stainless steel revolving stools and intimate red and white booths. The restaurant's menu was extensive including: sundaes, sodas, shakes, malts and an assortment of burgers. And, with the jukebox playing in the background, you could almost believe you had traveled back in time.

Mary glanced at the clock on the wall. She only had fifteen minutes to make it to her doctor's appointment, so Jodi was going to have to wait until tomorrow. *Ice cream,* she suddenly thought. *Ice cream sounds really good. Maybe I'll swing by after the appointment if I have time.*

Chapter Ten

Mary pulled the Roadster into a parking spot at the clinic on Kiwanis Avenue. She smiled when she saw the Police Cruiser parked a little further away. He made it and early!

A few minutes later they were sitting in an exam room with her doctor, Kristine Kelnick, an OB/GYN who was about Mary's age. She was also a marathon runner and it wasn't unusual to have her running shoes peeking out beneath her surgical scrubs at the hospital. Mary liked her open and forthright manner, and the fact that while she was in medical school working the graveyard shift she had had her own personal encounter with a ghost. It made life so much easier when your doctor didn't think you were nuts.

Dr. Kelnick pressed the screen on her tablet and accessed Mary's files. "You were in the hospital again?" she asked, her left eyebrow lifting slightly as she looked over the file. "Abrasions, slight concussion, bruising and…well this is interesting."

She looked at Mary over the tablet screen. "Did the hospital call you about any test results?" she asked.

Mary nodded and smiled. "Yes, the nurse called to tell me I was pregnant."

"Well, congratulations," Dr. Kelnick said. "And I'm assuming that's why you brought your own personal body-guard with you today."

"Exactly," Mary said.

Dr. Kelnick put the tablet on the countertop and pulled up a chair next to the examination table. "Okay, well we can run another pregnancy test," she said. "But I don't really think that's necessary at this point. It's too early into the pregnancy to hear a heartbeat or even detect the baby with an ultrasound; we've got to wait at least another month for that. If something happened to the baby on Saturday, you would see signs, spotting or bleeding. Anything like that happening?"

"No, nothing like that," Mary replied.

"Well, good," the doctor said with a smile. "Then you're still pregnant and there's no reason to assume that there's anything wrong."

"You mean everything's perfect with the baby?" Bradley asked.

"What I mean is, until this baby is a little older, we can't get any reliable data," she said. "So, instead of worrying and assuming the worst, you both need to be optimistic and enjoy this pregnancy. Fretting never helped anyone."

"So, what should I be doing?" Mary asked.

Dr. Kelnick met Mary's eyes and her eyebrow rose again. "You really need to stop getting into fights with serial killers," she said. "Do you think you can manage that for nine months or so?"

Mary nodded. "I'll leave all the serial killer fights to Bradley."

"You need to eat a sensible diet," she continued.

Mary sighed.

"What?" Dr. Kelnick asked.

"I had a call from Jodi at Union Dairy," Mary confessed. "I was going to go over there after this appointment. I mean, it was a work call, but I thought since I was there…"

"I said sensible, not restricted," the doctor said. "Ice cream, in moderation, is sensible."

Mary grinned. "I can be sensible."

"Exercise is important," she added. "But don't overdo it. Don't decide you need a new exercise regime now. Take it easy and listen to your body."

"I'm going to write you a prescription for prenatal vitamins," she continued. "Are you already feeling nauseous in the morning?"

Nodding, Mary placed her hand over her stomach. "Yes, all through the morning and sometimes in the afternoon."

"Well, these pills aren't going to help," she said with a smile. "If you can keep them down, great. But, don't torture yourself. If all you can do for now is eat a balanced diet and perhaps take some of those gummy vitamins, that's fine. At least those will stay in your body. But once the morning sickness ends, you need to take a prenatal vitamin every day."

"Okay, I can do that," Mary agreed. "Anything else?"

"Watch your carb intake," she said. "I don't mean you have to give up sugar, but gestational diabetes is not something we want to have to deal with. Once again, moderation is the key."

She picked up her tablet and jotted down a few notes. Then she looked up at them. "I want to see you back here in four weeks," she said. "In the meantime, just continue in your regular activities." She glanced at Bradley. "Including all normal marital relations."

Bradley nodded, but his cheeks were tinged with red.

"Call if you are concerned about anything," she said to Mary and then she left the room.

"That was slightly awkward," Bradley said once she was gone.

Laughing, Mary slid down from the table. "I don't know if I've seen you blush before."

"I didn't blush," he replied, standing up and putting his arms around her. "And I'm glad we can continue all our normal activities."

Wrapping her arms around his neck, she reached up and kissed him. "Me too," she murmured.

"So, shall we head home?" he asked, his arms loosely looped around her waist.

She paused for just a moment. "Well, I did want to stop by and see Jodi," she said.

"Because of the case or because of the ice cream?" he asked.

Mary bit her lower lip and bent her head. "A little of both," she admitted, and then she looked up at him. "Butter pecan sounds really good right now."

Laughing, he gave her a quick kiss. "I'll go pick Clarissa up at the Brennans and then start dinner," he said. "Take your time at Jodi's, but remember dinner will be ready when you get home, so…"

She nodded. "I know. Be sensible."

"Um, no, I was going to say 'bring some home,'" he said with a chuckle.

Chapter Eleven

The sky was beginning to darken when Mary parked her car in front of the ice cream parlor. The green neon lights that outlined the name of the store glowed in the early evening dusk. Even though it was early in the season, there were quite a few customers enjoying the fountain creations as Mary pushed open the glass door.

Glancing around, she saw Jodi behind the ice cream counter, scooping out a double scoop waffle cone. She headed over to the ice cream display to meet with Jodi and, if she was being honest with herself, to check out the newest flavors in the bins behind the glass window.

As soon as she walked over there, Jodi looked up from her scooping and nodded. "Hi Mary, thanks so much for coming by," she said. "I'll be with you in just a moment."

"Take your time," Mary insisted. "I'll just decide on what I want to bring home while you wait on your other customers."

She stepped closer to the display case to take a closer look at the choices and gasped in surprise when she got jostled in the side. She looked down to see a little boy standing next to her. "Sorry," he whispered. "I didn't mean to bump you."

His little freckled face was pressed up against the glass and his hands were plastered on either side of his face, so he could get an even better view. Mary was startled when the customer beside her walked through the little boy to hand a cluster of bills to Jodi to pay for her ice cream. The boy grinned up at Mary and shook his head. "That didn't hurt a bit," he said with a wide smile.

She looked around, there were far too many people close by for her to carry on a conversation with him. She met his eyes and returned his wink. "How come you can see me?" he asked.

She shrugged and smiled; frustrated that she couldn't talk to him without drawing attention to herself. Suddenly, a solution presented itself to her and she nearly slapped her forehead for not thinking of it sooner. She reached into her purse and pulled out her cell phone. Not dialing, she just held it to her ear and smiled down at the little boy. "Hi, I'm Mary O'Reilly," she said. "What's your name?"

"I'm Brandon," he replied. "Do you like ice cream?"

"I love it," she answered. "What's your favorite?"

He looked back at the dozens of choices and shook his head. "All of them," he finally said.

"Good answer," she said. "Do you come here often?"

"All the time," he said, and then he glanced quickly around. "Well, most afternoons when I'm not at the park or the library."

"Are you looking for someone?" she asked.

"My mom," he said with a soft sigh. "I've been looking for her for a long time and I just can't find her."

"Is that why you come here?" Mary asked. "To see if you can see her?"

Nodding, he looked around again. "We always came here together," he said. "But I haven't seen her for a long time."

"Can I help you find her?" Mary asked.

He shifted his gaze away from her. "Well, I'm not really supposed to talk with strangers," he said.

"You are exactly right," she said. "Strangers can be very dangerous. But I do want to help you find her. Perhaps I can look and bring her back here, so you wouldn't have to go anywhere with me."

Smiling, he met her eyes. "I bet that would work just fine," he said.

"Okay Brandon, I'll find her for you," she said. "In the meantime, now that we've met we aren't really strangers. So, if you need me, all you have to do is think about me and I'll be close by."

A woman standing close by turned to look at her and sent her an alarmed look.

Oops! Mary thought.

"Yes," she said aloud into the phone. "That's exactly how the story went. Crazy right?"

Brandon giggled. But Mary could see it did the trick and the woman was relieved.

"You're funny," he said. "Do you help people a lot?"

Mary shrugged. "Well, if I can," she said, lowering her voice. "And I especially like helping nice people who like ice cream. So, don't worry. I'll find your mom, okay?"

"Okay," he said, nodding enthusiastically. "Thanks for helping me."

"It's my pleasure," she said.

"Mary? Are you ready?" Jodi asked.

Mary glanced up at Jodi and took her phone away from her ear. "Sure, I just…" she turned and looked back, but Brandon was gone, so she quickly turned back. "I mean, sure, where do you want to meet?"

Mary followed Jodi back behind the counter and into a small office away from the restaurant.

74

"Have a seat," Jodi invited, gesturing to a metal folding chair. "Sorry it's not fancy."

Smiling, Mary shook her head. "No problem," she said, settling into the chair. "So, what's up?"

Seated on the other side of the desk, Jodi sat back in her chair and took a deep breath. "You know, if it was anyone but you, there would be no way I would say what I'm going to say," she said. "But, I figured you'd understand and even be able to help me." She paused for a moment. "And, of course, I want to pay you for your services."

"Why don't we worry about that later," Mary suggested. "Tell me why you called me."

"Well, I was working late in the office and I heard a noise out in the restaurant," Jodi said. "I figured it was one of my employees that had left something and so I went to see. I didn't bother turning on the light, because we have the streetlights and I didn't want anyone to think we were still open. I stepped right outside the office door."

Mary smiled inwardly, she was sure Jodi was going to tell her about Brandon and she would be able to tell her that she was already working on the case. She folded her arms happily across her chest. Finally, a mystery she had a jump on.

"...the woman," Jodi said.

Shaking her head and regretting her moment of woolgathering, she lifted her hand to stop Jodi. "I'm sorry, what did you say?"

"I said, that's when I saw the woman," Jodi repeated. "She was walking near the front counter and then she sat down on one of the stools. At first I was a little angry, you know, what the hell was someone doing in the restaurant at this hour? Which employee didn't lock the door behind them? But then..."

Jodi paused for a moment, stared at the office door and took a deep breath. "So, I stepped forward and immediately I felt the hairs standing up on the back of my neck. Like I knew intuitively something was wrong. I froze and looked at the woman again and I realized I could see through her, to the window behind her. Even before I could react, she looked at me, slowly shook her head and disappeared."

Turning to Mary, she shook her head once again. "I can tell you, it really freaked me out," she said. "But even more than being frightened, was the sense of sadness from her. When she looked at me, she seemed incredibly unhappy. I've heard... you know, small town, people talk...that you can somehow talk to ghosts."

Mary nodded. "Yes, I can do that," she replied.

"Could you…would you…talk to her and figure out what's wrong?"

"Yes, I'll be happy to do that," Mary said. "Do you want to be here when I talk to her?"

Shaking her head quickly, Jodi opened a desk drawer and pulled out a set of keys. "No, I really don't want to be here," she admitted. "Sorry, but once was enough for me."

Chuckling, Mary nodded. "I totally understand," she said. "Most people feel that way."

"So, what do I owe you for your services?" Jodi asked, pulling out a checkbook from the same drawer.

"How about a pint of butter pecan and a pint of Rocky Road?" Mary answered.

"Really? That's all?" Jodi asked.

"Well, if it takes a lot of time, I might need some dark chocolate brownie chunk," Mary added. "But we can discuss that later."

Jodi stood up and gave Mary a quick hug. "Thank you," she said. "I feel better already."

Chapter Twelve

"Hello, I'm home," Mary said as she opened the front door, juggling her purse, briefcase and three quarts of ice cream. Jodi had insisted on giving her a bonus.

"Hey, welcome home," Bradley said, as he walked out of the kitchen, wiping his hand on a kitchen towel.

He bent over and gave her a quick kiss on the cheek and relieved her of the items in her arms. "How are you feeling?" he whispered.

"Starving," she admitted and kissed him back. "I can't believe I practiced enough restraint to not eat all the ice cream on the way home."

"Jodi didn't give you a spoon. Right?" he asked with a smile.

She chuckled. "Exactly."

"Well, it's a good thing she didn't," he replied. "Rosie decided she needed to make dinner for us today and left a casserole of scalloped potatoes and ham, along with fresh rolls and a salad."

"Have I ever mentioned how much I love Rosie?" Mary asked, slipping off her coat and hanging it in the closet.

"She's a sweetheart," Bradley agreed, putting the items he had taken from Mary down on the table and then pulling her into his arms. "She also happened to mention that she owed you a favor for what you did for her this afternoon. Care to explain?"

"It was nothing, really," she said. "Rosie has a piece of property listed in the country. It's an adorable home on beautiful acreage, but people keep walking away. Rosie thought it might be haunted and people could feel it – so they walked away without placing an offer."

"And?" he asked.

Shrugging, Mary sighed. "Well, she was right," she said. "It looks like the former owner was murdered, but someone made it look like a farming accident."

"Can I just say, in a very typical male over-protective way, that I'm really not crazy about you investigating a murder," he said, pulling her close and laying his head on hers. "How about if you stop seeing ghosts for, say nine months or so, and instead do something safe and boring?"

Brandon's face immediately came to mind and she shook her head. "Sorry, I just can't," she said, wrapping her arms around his waist. "But I will be very careful and if I feel threatened in any way, I'll back off and call you."

79

Kissing her forehead, he stepped back and met her eyes. "You know I want to wrap you up in bubble wrap for the next nine months," he said.

"That's really kinky, Police Chief Alden," she replied with a quick smile. "But, you know, maybe later."

Laughing, he shook his head. "You know that's not what I meant," he said, then he paused and his smile turned slightly wicked. "Although, now that you mention it..."

"Mary, you're home," Clarissa called from the staircase.

Slipping out of Bradley's arms, she turned and looked across the room. Clarissa was hurrying down the stairs, with Mike close behind. "Mike helped me with my homework," Clarissa said. "He's real good at times tables."

"So far, so good," Mike replied. "I've remembered up through the sixes, I might have to start making stuff up when we hit the sevens and eights."

Clarissa giggled. "I'll just tell my teacher, my guardian angel said it was right."

Mike shook his head. "Don't do that," he said with a fake shudder, "it will give the rest of the guardian angels a bad name."

When Clarissa reached the final step, Mary was delighted when she ran to her and wrapped her arms around her. Mary enfolded her daughter in a warm hug. "Not only am I home," she whispered into her ear. "I brought ice cream from Union Dairy. Rocky Road."

"Really?" Clarissa asked, pulling slightly back with a wide smile on her face. "You're the best!"

"So, how was school today?" Mary asked.

"It was a little weird," Clarissa admitted. "I kept thinking a bad guy was going to come into my classroom and get me. And I was worried that Mike wouldn't be there if he came."

"Oh, sweetheart," Mary said, her heart dropping. "I'm so sorry. That must have been so frightening for you."

Nodding, Clarissa seemed to relax a little in Mary's arms. "It was scary," she admitted. "And even though I knew he was in jail, I had to keep looking at the door and the windows, just in case he got out."

Mike bent over. "You know I'd do everything I could to protect you," he said.

She nodded. "But what if something happens and you're not there, like when I took my bike and the bad man tried to catch me?" she asked.

Mike's face dropped and he sighed. "I couldn't help you then," he said. "Because of the choices you made. But other times, I'll be there."

"But what if you're not?" she asked.

Bradley squatted down next to Clarissa. "You've been through some pretty scary times, and even though we know the bad man is gone, it's hard not to think about it."

"Yes, my brain tells me he's gone, but my heart still jumps when someone comes in the door."

"Exactly," Bradley said. "That's a perfectly normal thing. And I had been thinking you might feel that way, so I bought you a present."

"A present?" Clarissa asked. "How can a present help me?"

Bradley stood up and walked across the room to his briefcase. He opened it and pulled out a little box. "First, you need to know that I trust Mike and I know he will do everything he can to protect you. He's part of our family and he loves you as much as Mary and I love you," Bradley said.

Clarissa shook her head. "Yeah, I know," she said, turning to her guardian angel. "Sorry Mike."

Mike shrugged. "That's okay, sweetheart," he said. "I'd be a little nervous too if I were you."

"And that's why we have this, to make you less nervous," Bradley said, pulling out a small plastic device. "It's a little GPS device that you can carry with you everywhere you go. It sends out a signal, that lets us know where you are all the time and it also has a button that you can push if you're scared that will alert us immediately. Would that be helpful?"

Clarissa took the small box in her hand. "This is so cool."

"Really?" Mary asked, looking at the device. "She's right, this is so cool."

Bradley nodded. "Yeah, I was just reading about it last week and thought it would be great for Clarissa," he said to Mary and then turned to his daughter. "What do you think?"

"I just push it when I need you?" she asked.

"Yes, just push it," Bradley replied. "And it will ring an alarm on both my phone and Mary's phone. Will that make you feel safer?"

"Yes. And I promise only to push it in emergencies," Clarissa said.

"And remember, pizza, hamburgers and ice cream are not emergencies," Mike added.

Clarissa giggled and then stopped. "Oh, ice cream," she said. "I almost forgot about the ice cream."

"I think we should eat dinner and then pig out on ice cream," Bradley suggested. "Anyone else interested?"

"Yes!" Mary and Clarissa agreed.

Chapter Thirteen

"You're going out tonight?" Bradley asked, later that night once Clarissa was tucked into bed. "Are you sure you're feeling up to it?"

"I'm fine," Mary said, slipping on her coat. "Besides, all I'll be doing is sitting in an ice cream parlor having a discussion with dead people. No big deal."

Bradley chuckled. "Do you think it's strange that I don't think that's strange?" he asked.

She walked over and kissed him. "Nope, because since you've met me, you're a changed man."

He kissed her back. "Changed for the better? Or just another step closer to crazy?"

She laughed. "For the better."

"How long will you be?"

"Not more than a couple of hours," she replied.

"Okay, if something comes up, call me. I can get Katie or Clifford to run over if you need my help," he said. "I've got some paperwork I can work on while you're gone."

"Great! See you soon," she said.

The moon was bright and full. The night air was cool with just a hint of spring. Mary took a deep breath as she walked to the car, inhaling the moist scents of damp earth and spring flowers. She paused for a second, savoring the fragrance of a nearby hyacinth. She really loved spring.

The drive back to Union Dairy only took a few minutes. The downtown streets were fairly deserted by this time of night, except for the Lindo Theater a few blocks down Chicago. Mary parked directly in front of the ice cream parlor, slipped out of her car and pulled the keys Jodi had given her out of her pocket. She paused at the plate glass door and stared inside for a moment before entering. The restaurant was motionless and quiet, with the only light coming from the glow of some of the equipment behind the counter. Everything else lay in shadows.

Slipping the key in, she slowly turned it and opened the door. Entering the building, she locked the door behind her to ensure she didn't have any company of the human kind. She walked forward to the short counter with the bright red parlor stools that surrounded it. The counter snaked around from the front of the restaurant around a curve at the side and then along the back of the front area, so a soda jerk could stand in the middle and take care of all of the customers around him. The second dining area was a smaller room with a collection of tables and booths for people who wanted a little more privacy than the counter afforded. Between the two rooms was a small alcove that held an old jukebox with tunes from earlier years. Customers from either side of the restaurant could enjoy the music for only a quarter.

The restaurant was warm; Mary was sure Jodi had left the heat up for her comfort, so she slipped off her coat and laid it on the red Formica counter. She glanced around the room. Light glinted off the chrome fixtures behind the counter and the lines of sparkling sundae and shake glasses on the shelves. Mary started when she thought she saw someone behind the counter, but released a soft breath when she realized it was only her reflection in the mirror on the wall.

The sounds of the night were different than the sounds during the day. The freezer hummed softly, the ice maker thumped and the furnace occasionally whooshed as it started a new cycle. There was no clattering of silverware, no chattering of customers, no clinking of dishware or ringing of the cash register. It was as if the restaurant were asleep, breathing deeply, waiting for someone to wake it up.

Mary slid onto a short stool; making sure to avoid the one Jodi said had been occupied by the ghost. She couldn't help herself; she twisted the seat from one side to the other, enjoying the movement just as much today as she did when she was a child. She was about to laugh out loud when a new noise stopped her.

87

Cha-ching. The jukebox suddenly lit up. She could hear the sounds of the mechanism lifting the record from its shelf and moving it over to the player. Then the voices of the Everly Brothers singing *"Whenever I Want You All I Have to do is Dream"* echoed throughout the room. The figure of a young woman slowly materialized in front of the jukebox, swaying to the music. She was dressed in a plaid cotton shirtdress with a full skirt and a matching cardigan sweater draped over her shoulders. She looked like she stepped out of a movie from the fifties, from her shoulder length hair, styled in soft waves and bangs, to her ballerina-style flats.

Mary just sat and watched the girl as a frisson of paranormal electricity swept up her back and along her arms. As the song ended, the girl turned and walked toward the counter, perching on the stool next to Mary. The pedestal stool slowly turned, but instead of the quiet, well-oiled stool Mary was on, the mechanism squealed painfully. In a moment, Mary was face to face with the specter. "Hi," Mary said, "I'm Mary."

The ghost stared at her for a moment and then slowly smiled. "Hi Mary, I'm Erika," she replied. "Do have any smokes?"

Shaking her head, Mary said, "Sorry, I don't smoke."

"That's okay," Erika replied evenly. "The guys will be along soon and they always have them."

"The guys?" Mary asked.

"Yeah, you know, for cruising," she said. "I'm dying to ride in Adam's Chevy, it's dreamy."

"Cruising?" Mary asked.

"What are you from outer space or something?" Erika asked.

"Yeah, well, I'm from Chicago originally."

Erika's face brightened considerably. "You're from Chicago? That is just dreamy," she said. "I bet you hate it here in Freeport. There is absolutely nothing here compared to Chicago. Do you know any gangsters?"

"No, sorry, my family is in law enforcement," Mary replied.

"Oh, that's too bad," Erika said.

"So, you were telling me about cruising," Mary prompted.

"Oh, ya, sure," Erika said. "The boys drive their cars downtown and they pick the girls who get to ride in their cars, unless, of course, they got a steady."

"A steady?" Mary asked.

"They don't teach you a lot in Chicago," Erika said, rolling her eyes. "You know, a steady, like a boyfriend and a girlfriend. Going together. A steady."

"Oh, got it," Mary said. "So, if they don't have a steady, they pick up the girls and let them ride in their car."

"Exactly," Erika said and she added with a small smile. "Or they have a secret steady and they both act like they're free."

"And where do they go?"

"They just drive, up and down Galena," she said.

"Just up and down the same road?" Mary asked.

"Yes, it's called cruising," Erika replied. "We cruise the drag."

"Why?"

"So people can see us and we can see other people."

"Couldn't you just all see each other here at the ice cream parlor?"

"Are you from this century?" Erika asked.

Mary just smiled. "Sorry, I guess it's a new concept to me. It sounds like fun," she tried to sound enthusiastic. "It's just seems like a waste of gasoline."

Shrugging, Erika spun on her stool. "So, it's only a quarter a gallon," she said. "No big deal."

"A quarter a gallon," Mary repeated. "Wow."

"You sound like my dad," the ghost replied. "He says that's highway robbery."

Then Erika peered past Mary and sighed.

"What's wrong?" Mary asked.

"He's late again," she said, her face dropping. "He promised he'd be here."

She stood up and walked to the plate glass door and peered out.

Mary followed her to the window. "Erika, how long have you been waiting for him?"

Erika paused, considering Mary's question. Finally she turned to her. "I think I've been waiting a long time," she said, her voice dropping to a whisper. "A very long time."

"A very, very long time."

Then she faded away before Mary's eyes.

Chapter Fourteen

Mary sat in the dark restaurant for short while longer, hoping to catch another glimpse of Brandon. But as the wall clock echoed loudly in the relative quiet and the various machines went through their cycles, no other supernatural event occurred. Finally, Mary placed her hands on the counter, pushed herself up and walked across the darkened ice cream parlor to the front door. Turning, she took one last look around the large room. Everything was still and in place for the next morning. Shrugging, she unlocked the door and stepped outside to the street. Maybe Brandon and Erika would contact her at home, now that they'd made a connection with her.

Locking the door behind her, she hurried to her car and drove back in the quiet streets to her home.

"So, how'd it go?" Bradley asked her as she walked into the house. "Did you make any new friends today?"

Chuckling, she nodded. "Yes, as a matter of fact, I did," she replied, slipping her coat off and hanging in the closet. "I met Erika, a teenager from the fifties. She was waiting for someone to take her cruising, but they never showed up."

He turned from the desk he was sitting behind. "She's been waiting a long time," he said.

"Yeah, I hate when dates go that way," she said. "You wait for half a century and they still don't show up. That's just plain rude if you ask me."

Standing, he walked over and wrapped his arms around her. "I'm sure you never had to worry about being stood up for a date," he said, placing a kiss on her head.

She looked up at him with disbelief on her face. "Excuse me?" she asked. "I do recall sitting around in a sexy black dress for several hours while my date was otherwise occupied."

"Well, there was a train derailment," he said.

"Oh, yeah, the old train derailment excuse," she teased. "I've heard that one a hundred times."

He pulled her closer. "I promise you I would have much preferred to be in the company of you and that sexy black dress," he murmured, trailing kisses down the side of her face. "But, as I recall, I did make up for it later."

She turned her face, so her lips met his. "Oh, yes, you did," she whispered just before she kissed him back.

Lifting her into his arms, he carried her to the staircase. "Why don't we continue this discussion upstairs?" he suggested, his voice slightly rough with emotion.

Mary snuggled closer. "Excellent idea."

Sometime later Mary lay next to Bradley, her head nestled in the crook of his shoulder and his arms wrapped around her. "Well, this was a great day," she sighed contentedly.

He leaned over and placed a kiss on her forehead. "Yes it was," he answered. "I still can't believe it. A baby."

She smiled softly and slipped her hand down over her still flat abdomen. "I know how you feel," she replied. "I can't believe it either."

"When do you want to tell your family?" he asked.

"I really think I want to wait until we're sure," she replied. "After the first trimester. Is that okay with you?"

"Yes, that sounds fine. You know, I've been thinking that the baby ought to have an amazing and distinct name," Bradley said. "Perhaps a family name."

"That's a great idea," she said. "I love the idea of a family name. Any ones come to mind?"

"Well, I have a great aunt Berengaria, she's named after a thirteenth century queen," he suggested.

"Berengaria?" Mary asked, not quite believing her ears.

"Yes, Great Aunt Beren," he replied.

"Okay, well, that's one name we can cross off the list," Mary stated.

"We could call her Gari," he suggested.

"Let me think about that," she said, and then before less than two seconds passed added. "No."

"Okay, well, if we have a boy, I have a great-great uncle Eustace," he said.

Mary rolled over to her side and gently placed her hand on Bradley's lips. "So, what you are trying to tell me is that if we choose a family name, we're using my family."

She could feel the rumble of laughter in his chest, although he tried to keep a straight face. "Okay, you try to do better than Eustace and Berengaria," he challenged.

"Oh, well, that's easy," she replied with a twinkle in her eyes. "There's my cousin, Drizella, a lovely girl who lives in County Cork."

"Didn't she try to kill a bunch of Dalmatian puppies?" he asked.

"That was Cruella," Mary pointed out. "Not Drizella."

"Oh, well, that's much better," he said. "And for a boy?"

"Well, I have a great-great uncle Porick," she suggested.

Bradley shook his head. "Like bacon?"

"That's pork, not Por-ick," she explained.

"But when he's little and tells someone his name, it's going to sound like we named him after the other white meat, right?"

"Okay, maybe," Mary agreed with a sigh, rolling back and snuggling against him. "This is going to be harder than I thought."

"Yeah, and maybe we stay away from family names," Bradley suggested, "For the sake of the baby."

Mary giggled. "I agree."

Chapter Fifteen

Mary opened her eyes and waited, doing a mental inventory of her physical status. *Stomach feels fine*, she decided, *no lightheadedness, no nausea and I really have to go to the bathroom. I think I'm good.*

Slipping out from beneath the blankets, she hurried to the bathroom, optimistic that her bout with morning sickness was over. But once she was on her feet for a few minutes, her stomach clenched and she bent over the toilet.

Twenty minutes later she was showered, dressed and heading towards the staircase. She was actually feeling hungry. This was going to be a great day. She placed her foot on the first step and stopped. What was that smell?

"Hey, good morning sunshine," Mike said, appearing next to her. "Taking it a little easy this morning?"

She smiled wanly at him and nodded. "Yes, I'm, uh…"

The scent of the food drifted upward and she caught a full whiff. Green peppers and onions? Her stomach spun and she clapped a hand over her mouth, dashing back down the hall to her bedroom.

"Hey, what's wrong?" Mike asked, chasing after her. "Are you okay?"

"Mmmph," she muttered, racing through her room to the bathroom. She made it to the toilet just in time.

"Oh, gross," Mike said, gliding into the bathroom and gliding quickly out. He stood on the outside of the doorway and cringed. "Hey, are you okay?"

Mary gagged again.

"I'll take that as a no," he replied. "Do you want me to get Bradley?"

"No…I'm fine," she whispered weakly.

Cautiously, he ventured into the bathroom. "Are you okay?"

She straightened up and grabbed a bottle of mouthwash, pouring out cap full and swishing it around in her mouth. Finally, she spit it out, breathed a sigh, leaned back against the wall and patted her face with a hand towel. "How do I look?" she asked.

"Like a woman who just emptied her entire stomach cavity into the toilet," he said moving closer and demanding, "What's wrong with you?"

"Morning sickness," she said.

"What the hell is…," he paused and the concern on his face slowly turned into a grin. "Really? Morning sickness? Like having a crying, screaming, little brat in nine months kind of sickness?"

She smiled back and nodded. "Yep, just like that."

"Wow," he replied, a wide smile on his face. "That's so cool! What are you having?"

"A baby," she said. "I thought we just established that."

"No, I mean, yes we did. But which kind, a boy kind or a girl kind?"

"Oh. It's too early to know about that yet," she said, putting her hands on her abdomen. "Just a baby kind."

"So, should you be up?" he asked, starting to panic. "Can I get you a chair or a blanket or something?"

Chuckling, she shook her head and took a deep breath. "Well, if you could remove the smell of peppers and onions from the house, that would be amazing," she said. "I find I'm a little sensitive to odors."

"Ah, Bradley was making your favorite breakfast, breakfast burritos with chorizo," he replied.

Mary clapped a hand back over her mouth and took a deep breath, counting slowly to ten.

Mike waited. "You okay?"

After another deep breath, Mary nodded. "Yeah, I'm fine."

"Hey, you stay up here for another couple of minutes," he said. "I'll run interference in the kitchen. How does herb tea to go sound?"

"That and a package of soda crackers sounds perfect," she said.

"You've got it," he said with a quick smile before he disappeared. Immediately, he reappeared. "Hey, by the way, congratulations."

"Thanks, Mike."

He faded away once more. And once more, he reappeared. "Uh, I'm guessing Bradley knows, but how about Clarissa?"

"Oh, thanks for asking," she replied. "No, she doesn't know yet. We're waiting for the right time."

"Got it!" He faded away and Mary held her breath, waiting for him to reappear. After a few minutes, she figured he was downstairs, delivering her message. Taking a deep breath, she left the bathroom and hurried down the stairs where Bradley was standing next to the bottom step with a covered mug in one hand and a paper sack in the other.

"Hey," he smiled at her. "Sorry about the breakfast surprise, I wasn't thinking."

"It was really sweet of you," she said. "But, I'm feeling that it's more of a crackers and herb tea morning."

"Are you sick?" Clarissa asked as she dug into her burrito.

Mary could barely look at the forkful of thick melted cheese and eggs in Clarissa's hand. Taking another deep breath, she shook her head quickly and smiled. "Just a queasy stomach," she said. "That's all."

Bradley put his arm around her and walked her to the front door. "I'll air out the kitchen before I go to work, so you don't have green peppers and onions greeting you when you get home," he said. "And I'll make lunch for Clarissa. I'm thinking any sandwich combination she'd like might kick morning sickness into overdrive."

"You wouldn't mind?" she asked.

He shook his head. "No, Clarissa and I are fine," he said. "Why don't you head to the office where it doesn't smell like a taco place?"

She leaned up and kissed his cheek. "Thanks, I think I will," she said. "Did you tell Clarissa about Dr. Springler?"

"No, I haven't done that yet," he said. "Would you like me to mention it once you're gone?"

Sipping on the tea, she felt her stomach calm a little. "No, we should do it together," she said. "I think I'm fine right now."

She walked back across the room and stood by the table. "Clarissa," she called. "We have an appointment this afternoon with Dr. Karen Springler."

"Who's she?" Clarissa asked.

"She's a lovely lady who talks to people about their feelings," Mary said. "And she helps families figure out how to be happier."

"I thought we were happy," Clarissa replied, a shadow of concern crossing over her face. "I'm trying to do better."

Mary slipped into the chair next to Clarissa and Bradley strategically moved Clarissa's plate further away, earning a grateful smile from Mary.

"You are doing a great job," Mary said to Clarissa. "And we love you so much. But we realize that a lot has happened to all of us, especially you, during these past few months. Dr. Springler is the kind of doctor that helps us fix some of the hurts and worries we have on the inside."

Clarissa glanced at Bradley and Mike, and then back at Mary. "Are we all going to talk to her?" she asked.

Mary nodded. "The first time we meet, we all get to talk to her and explain how we feel," she said. "But then we also get to meet with her individually, in case there are things we need to talk about that we don't want someone else to hear. Dr. Springler is very good at keeping secrets."

"If you don't mind, I'll stay home," Mike said. "But, Clarissa, if you ever need to talk to someone, I'm your guy. And if you want me to go with you, I can do that too."

Sitting quietly for a few moments, Clarissa seemed to be contemplating the conversation. Finally she looked up at her parents. "But we're still good?" she asked. "We still love each other?"

Bradley reached down and kissed Clarissa on the top of her head. "We are great," he said. "But we want to be even better because we want our family to last forever. And Dr. Springler can help us learn how to communicate even better and get closer together."

"Okay, that sounds good," she agreed.

"Great," Mary said. "Your dad will pick you up after school today, so don't get on the bus. I'll call the school and remind them."

"Okay," Clarissa said and then she smiled up at Bradley. "Can we drive with the sirens on?"

Bradley shook his head. "No, sorry, sweetheart," he replied. "Sirens are only for emergencies."

Mary bent forward and gave Clarissa a kiss. "Good try though," she whispered with a smile and Clarissa laughed.

"I'll see you both later," Mary added, and then she grabbed her coat and briefcase as she hurried out of the house.

Unlocking the car door, she quickly sat in the front seat of the Roadster and breathed deeply for a few moments while another wave of nausea passed. Finally, she ripped open the sleeve of crackers, shoved one in her mouth and crunched down. "Oh, yeah, this is going to be fun," she muttered before putting the car in gear and driving away.

Chapter Sixteen

"Protein," Rosie said, marching into Mary's office and dropping a small bag on the top of her desk.

"Protein?" Mary asked.

Rosie nodded. "Yes, protein first thing in the morning helps you overcome morning sickness."

Mary unwrapped the brown paper sack and looked inside. There were several small plastic bags filled with cubes of cheese or meat. She pulled one out that was filled with yellow cubes of cheese, opened it and sniffed.

"Oh, that was my favorite," Rosie said. "Aged cheddar. That set my stomach to right most mornings."

Reaching in, Mary pulled out a square and popped it into her mouth. The cheese nearly melted in her mouth, the sharp taste actually settling her stomach. "This is good," she said, pulling out another piece and putting it in her mouth.

"Just take it easy," Rosie warned. "A piece at a time, just to be sure your stomach really likes it and isn't messing with your mind."

"My stomach will mess with my mind?"

Nodding sagely, Rosie sat in the chair across from Mary. "Oh, yes, pregnancy pretty much turns your whole body into foreign territory—intense cravings, rollercoaster emotions, acne, hair loss, exhaustion, insomnia. And that's just the start."

Mary sat back in her chair and stared at Rosie, her eyes wide with shock. "You can't be serious. Why does anyone get pregnant a second time?"

Rosie's smiled warmed. "Because once you hold your baby in your arms, you forget about all of the little annoyances. You know you've just taken part in a miracle and the rest doesn't seem to matter anymore."

Mary pulled out another bag; this one filled with cubes of chicken, picked up a cube and bit it. "Protein, huh?" she asked.

Nodding, Rosie grinned. "You've got it."

"So, what else do you have for me this morning?" Mary asked, picking up another cube of chicken and actually feeling much better.

"I brought the real estate contracts you asked me about yesterday," she said, pulling out a manila folder filled with paper. "It looks like the property was sold soon after Dale's death."

Mary took the proffered folder and looked through the paperwork. "It was all sold to a large corporate farming organization, Maughold

International," Mary said. "Are you familiar with them?"

Nodding her head, Rosie peered over the desk to look at the paperwork. "Yes, they were pretty active around here about fifteen years ago. They wanted to put in some big mega-dairy farms and the community was up in arms because they worried about the possibility of water contamination from so many animals on a relatively small tract of land."

"So what happened?"

"Well, the county board finally voted it down," Rosie explained. "The company was pretty upset because they had gone around purchasing a bunch of land assuming they had the county board's approval."

Mary looked up from the paperwork. "Sounds like an inside deal gone wrong," she surmised.

Rosie nodded. "There was a lot of speculation about that," she said. "Especially in the real estate profession. Those land brokers who were buying up for Maughold were pretty upset. And the broker from Chicago, Quinn Edmonson —the one that dated Dale's daughter for a while—lost his job."

"Quinn Edmonson," Mary mused. "Why do I know that name?"

"Because once they fired him, he was left high and dry and stuck here in Freeport," Rosie said.

"One of the local bank presidents—the one who held the Maughold accounts for a while— felt sorry for him and gave him a job."

"Okay, that's how I know him," Mary said. "I think I've met him at a couple of Chamber of Commerce Meet and Greets. He seemed nice enough."

"Well, for a while he had more enemies than friends in town," Rosie said. "But it's been fifteen years, so some people have forgiven him."

"How did the Johnson property figure into the Maughold project?"

"I'm not sure," Rosie admitted. "I've asked the county recorder for some older Platte maps so we can determine the Johnson holdings before the sale and after. It should also show us the properties Maughold had in the area."

Nodding, Mary shuffled the papers back into the folder. "So, the next step is to interview the family members. How do you want me to handle it?"

Sitting back in her chair, Rosie pondered Mary's question for a few minutes. "I suppose if we are considering one of the children as possible murderers, we shouldn't tell them we are looking into their father's death, should we?"

"No, that wouldn't be a good idea," Mary agreed, laying a protective hand on her stomach. "I don't want to put either of us in jeopardy."

"I could tell them that you are interested in purchasing the property, but you had some questions about the history of the farm," Rosie suggested. "I could introduce you to Greta and see where we go from there."

"Is there a way I can get a key to the house?" Mary asked. "I'd like to talk to Dale…"

Mary stopped talking when Dale appeared behind Rosie's chair in her office.

"I got the feeling someone was talking about me," he said, slowly gazing around her office. "I thought about our conversation and suddenly I was here. How did that happen?"

"You and I are connected now," Mary said.

"Why of course we're connected, but I don't see what that has to do with getting you a key," Rosie said, confused at Mary's statement.

"Rosie, Dale just joined us," Mary replied.

Sitting up in her chair and glancing around the room, Rosie whispered, "I can't see him."

Dale grinned. "She does know I'm a ghost, right?"

Mary smiled at him and nodded. "Rosie, he's still a ghost, but he's right behind your chair."

"Oh, of course," Rosie replied, turning in her chair to face the space behind her. "I am so sorry about your untimely death and I do hope we can get to the bottom of everything."

Dale's grin softened to a rueful smile. "She's a nice lady, isn't she?" he asked.

"She's the salt of the earth," Mary answered.

Rosie turned back to Mary. "Who? Who else is here?" she asked.

"You are the salt of the earth," Mary said. "And no one else is here, just you, Dale and me."

Turning back again to face the empty space, Rosie said, "We were just talking about your murder and how to proceed."

"Rosie," Mary gasped.

"That's okay," Dale said. "She's just calling a spade a spade, no mincing words. I like that."

"I'm sorry," Rosie said. "Did I say something wrong?"

"Not wrong," Mary replied. "Just very directly."

"Oh, I didn't realize…," she began, and then started again. "I'm sorry. What I meant to say is we were just talking about…well…your um…"

Rosie sighed loudly and looked at Mary. "Well, really Mary, the man knows he's dead and he knows he's a ghost. I don't see why we just don't call a spade a spade and say the word murder."

Dale shook his head sadly. "She's exactly right," he agreed. "I was murdered and, unfortunately, the most likely suspects are my children."

"So, how would you like us to proceed?" Mary asked.

Chapter Seventeen

Mary had visited the nursing home near Krape Park a number of times. It was a lovely, upscale facility with a staff that catered to the more affluent members of Freeport's elderly community. The sale of the farmland had been a good thing for Greta, Mary thought as she walked down the polished wood floors past expensive antique furniture. Stopping at the front desk she greeted the young receptionist who had helped her a number of times. "Hello, Jennika," she said. "How are you today?"

"I'm great, Miss O'Reilly. How are you?"

"Well, actually, I'm not Miss O'Reilly any longer," she replied with a smile. "I'm Mary Alden."

"As in Police Chief Alden?" she asked, her eyes and her smile widening. "Good job! He's a hunk."

Mary laughed and nodded. "Yes he is," she said. "And thank you."

"So, who do you need to see today?" Jennika asked.

"Greta Johnson," Mary said. "I think she's new here."

Nodding, Jennika scanned the computer screen in front of her. "Yes, she is and she's a sweetheart," she replied, and then looking up she handed Mary a guest badge and the sign-in clip board. "She's in room 112. All you need to do is go down this hallway to the right and knock on 112."

"Thanks for your help," Mary said, clipping on the badge after signing her name. "Is there anything I should know about her before going in?"

"Well, I can't divulge any official health information about her," Jennika said. "But if you are going in to talk to her, you're going to discover she doesn't have any filters. She will say whatever is on her mind and it can be a little shocking sometimes. But, for the most part, she's lucid."

"Well, I can't wait to meet her," Mary said with a smile and walked down the hall towards the room.

"What the hell is Greta doing in a place like this?" Dale asked, as he appeared next to Mary.

He gazed up and down the hall and shook his head in disgust. "She's a farm girl," he said. "She shouldn't be cooped up in here."

"Well, I'll be sure to ask her," Mary whispered, making sure no one was around to witness her speaking to thin air.

113

She tapped lightly on the door and in a moment the door was opened by a petite woman with silver hair and bright blue eyes.

"She's still beautiful," Dale said as he glided into the room.

"Hello, Mrs. Johnson," Mary said. "My name is Mary Alden. Rosie Wagner suggested I meet with you."

Greta smiled warmly. "Well, of course," she said, opening her door and inviting Mary in. "She called and told me you are interested in my house. Are you really interested? You seem awfully citified to be living in the country."

"No, I'm interested," Mary replied. "It's a lovely place."

Greta led her to a small dining room table placed near a window that overlooked the manicured grounds. "Please sit down. I'm so glad you like my house," she said with a soft sigh. "I raised my family there and I have so many fond memories."

"See, what did I tell you?" Dale growled. "They forced her in here."

"Are you regretting your move here?" Mary asked.

"Oh, no, dear," Greta said, placing her soft fragile hand over Mary's hand. "I was so lonely in that big house all by myself. It was a wonderful place to raise a family, but it's too empty when you're all alone. I love being here. There's so much to do and I have so many friends. And I learn the most interesting things about my neighbors."

Dale snorted. "She's just saying that."

"Even if I don't sell the house, I'll still be able to stay here," she added. "Dale left me very well-off. I don't think he would have been happy here, he so loved the farm and the land. But I would love to see another family in there. Rosie mentioned that you encountered some troubles when you were looking into the deed for the house."

"Yes, for some reason there is a lien on the house," Mary said, as she shuffled through her purse and brought out some papers. "The deed search shows a lien issued by Rogers Construction."

Greta shook her head in dismay. "I know that Steve Rogers did some work for us, years and years ago," she said. "But there has to be some mistake, we paid him for the work. Of course, he was always forgetful and he didn't do a very good job running his business either. I remember he did some plumbing work for us, disconnected the pipes to the sink, but forgot to turn off the water first. What a mess it was."

She paused for a moment. "I am positive we paid him, even though Dale thought he should have paid us for all the trouble he caused. Do you think that was it?"

"Well, sometimes contractors put the lien papers in, as a hold until they are paid," Mary said. "As you suggested, he might have just forgotten to take it off. Is there a way to contact him?"

"No, he died several years ago. I think it was a heart attack as I recall," Greta said. "I don't know how in the world we are going to work this out."

"This is great," Dale said. "Now she'll have you contact the kids."

"Do you have any family who might remember the situation?" Mary asked. "Perhaps I could talk with them and we could come up with a way to figure it out."

"Oh, that's a great idea," Greta said. "They are all much better at dealing with business situations than I am. They all say I chatter far too much. Let me write down their phone numbers for you, and then I'll give them all a call and tell them to expect your call. I'm sure we'll be able to figure this out."

"Thank you so much, Mrs. Johnson," Mary said. "I really do love your house."

"It's a wonderful home for a family," Greta said. "I do hope we can work this all out so you can buy it. I would be very happy knowing you are living there. My husband and I were very happy there."

"Yes we were," Dale agreed softly. "Very happy there."

"If you don't mind me asking, what happened to your husband?" Mary asked.

Greta sighed deeply and sat back against her chair. "He was killed in a farm accident," she said sadly.

"I'm so sorry," Mary replied.

"It was terrible," Greta said, turning to stare unseeing out the window. "Somehow he was trapped in a grain bin during harvest. He suffocated."

She turned back and met Mary's eyes. "I always wondered about his death," she confessed. "He was too smart to close a bin door behind him. He was always so careful about proper procedure. I just have never been able to bring myself to consider it an accident."

"Well, that's my Greta," Dale said. "She was always the smart one."

"Do you think it might not have been an accident?" Mary asked.

"Well, now, that's a problem, isn't it," Greta sad softly. "If I think Dale was killed, then who would have done the killing? I've watched those television murder mysteries for years, Mrs. Alden. I understand what motivates people and I pray to God every night that one of my children wasn't so overcome with greed that they decided to remove the one person that stood between them and a small fortune."

"With those suspicions in your mind, how do you continue to carry on a relationship with your children?" Mary asked.

Greta shrugged. "It hasn't been easy," she admitted. "I try to love them and accept them, but always in the back of my mind, there's a little fear, a little doubt. We haven't been all that close since Dale died, especially Abe."

"Abe? Why is that?" Mary asked.

"He was the one driving the truck that night," Greta explained. "He was the one who used the auger to feed the grain from the truck into the top of the bin. It looks like Dale was pounding on the door, screaming for help, but Abe was wearing protective hearing gear because the machinery is so loud, so he never heard him."

"Abe blames himself for his father's death?" Mary asked.

"He doesn't talk about it," Greta said. "He doesn't touch the money he got from the sale of the land. He pretty much keeps to himself."

"Damn it," Dale swore. "Abe was such a hard-working and good boy; I wouldn't want my death to ruin his life."

"Do you think Abe could have done it?" Mary asked.

Greta shook her head. "I've lived with these suspicions for over fifteen years. I don't want to think any of my children would have done it," she said. "But I also wonder if perhaps it's remorse rather than guilt that keeps Abe away."

"Tell her what you do," Dale insisted. "Tell her about me. Tell her you're going to look into my death."

Mary stood and smiled at Greta. "Thank you so much for your time," she said. "I'll contact your children about the lien."

Greta clasped Mary's hands in her own. "Thank you, Mary," she said. "I hope you can figure this all out."

"So do I," Mary said earnestly. "So do I."

She let herself out of the room and looked both ways down the hall to be sure she was alone.

"Why didn't you tell her?" Dale demanded.

"Because she could have said no," Mary whispered.

"What?"

"Dale, she's had these feelings about your death ever since you died," Mary said. "It's only her current condition that allows her to speak of her feelings. She is protecting her children, she would never agree to me investigating them. And if she called them and told them I was investigating things, do you think they'd be as forthcoming as I need?"

Sighing, Dale shook his head. "No, I suppose you're right," he said. "And Greta is right. I hate to think one of our children could kill me."

"Unfortunately, it happens every day," Mary said. "But, don't give up on your children yet. We haven't even begun to investigate."

Chapter Eighteen

Mary walked into the lobby of the bank in downtown Freeport. The building itself was old, but the lobby had been recently remodeled and had a warm and welcoming feeling to it. The reception desk was staffed by a friendly young man who immediately looked up when Mary walked through the doors.

"Hello, can I help you?"

"Hi, I was wondering if I could speak with Quinn Edmonson," she said. "I don't have an appointment, I was just hoping he'd be free."

"Let me check," he replied, picking up the phone and punching in a few numbers on the switchboard.

Mary walked over to the cozy waiting area and settled down on an overstuffed chair near the fireplace. But she didn't have a chance to get too comfortable, a moment later a middle-aged man came over and greeted her. "Hi, I'm Quinn," he said, extending his hand.

Mary stood and shook his hand. "Hi, I'm Mary O'Reilly," she said, using her business name. "I think we've met at some Chamber events."

He nodded. "Yes, I remember," he said. "You do private investigation work, right?"

"Yes, I do," she said. "And I'm actually working on a local case right now. Could I meet with you for a few minutes and ask you some questions?"

"Okay, but I can't divulge any private banking information without some kind of a warrant," he cautioned, still leading her into his private office off the lobby.

She shook her head. "Oh, no, this has to do with your work before you were employed by the bank," she said.

Closing the door, he offered her a chair and then walked around and sat on the other side of the desk. Templing his hands, he met her eyes. "Before I was employed by the bank?" he asked. "When I was working for Maughold?"

"Yes, that's right," she said. "I'm doing a real estate investigation, nothing too tricky. There appears to be a lien on some property and Maughold purchased some of the adjoining land. I was hoping you could remember if you had a lien issue too."

"I don't remember any lien issues," he said. "But maybe if I knew the owners of the property…"

"Of course," Mary said with a smile, waiting to see his reaction when she offered the name. "The last name was Johnson. The original owner was Dale Johnson."

Several emotions flashed across his face before he was able to school his emotions. There was regret, sadness and a little anger. Finally he nodded. "Yes, I actually remember the Johnson farm well. There was no lien on the property when we purchased it," he said.

"Are you sure?" Mary asked. "I mean, I'm sure you worked with so many different farmers."

"Actually, I got to know the family quite well, so I would remember this one," he said. "As a matter of fact, Jessie Johnson and I were dating."

"Oh, how nice," Mary replied. "I'm not working for the Johnson family, I've been hired by someone who is interested in the house, but I understand they are lovely people."

"They're lovely unless they suspect you of murder," he muttered.

"Pardon me," Mary asked, but she had heard every word.

"Nothing. It was nothing," he replied. "After Dale passed away, I dealt primarily with Josh, the oldest son. He wanted to liquidate the property quickly. Much faster than the rest of his family wanted to move."

"Why the rush?"

Quinn sat back in his chair. "Well…," he paused and studied Mary. "This is confidential, right?"

"Absolutely," Mary said.

"The county board was going to vote on allowing the Maughold project to go through or not at the next board meeting," he said. "Farmers were offered an incentive to sell before the vote in order to encourage the board's positive reaction to the project. The Johnson land was a keystone property in the whole project, if we didn't have their land, we really didn't have a project. So, let's say Josh was given an incentive, a nice incentive, to sign quickly."

"But the whole family got their share, right?" Mary asked. "It wasn't only incentive for Josh?"

"No, Josh split the money evenly," he replied. "But if he had waited a little longer, like the rest of the family wanted, there would have been no sale. The board voted down the project and the land's value dropped to one tenth of what Maughold was willing to pay for it."

"One tenth?" Mary asked, astonished.

"Yes. And if poor Dale Johnson hadn't had his farming accident when he did, the family would still be eking out a living as farmers rather than living the high life they now enjoy."

"If you don't mind me saying," Mary inserted. "You sound a little bitter."

He sighed. "I really cared for Jessie, actually I loved her," he said. "But it was my job to push Josh to sign. It was my job to do everything I could to see the project through completion. But I wouldn't have killed someone for it and I have to say, I got the feeling that she had her suspicions after he died."

"Did she ever accuse you?"

He shook his head. "No, because if they claimed it was something more than an accident there would have been an investigation," he said. "And if it wasn't me, then it might have been her sainted brother."

"Do you really think he could have murdered his father for money?" she asked.

"I don't know," he said. "I really don't. But people have done worse for a lot less."

Suddenly the alarm on Mary's phone went off and she jumped. "Oh, I'm sorry," she said. "It startled me."

She looked down and saw the appointment reminder for the psychologist. "I'm so sorry, I have to run," she said. "But I want to thank you for the information about the Johnson farm. You've been very helpful."

125

He stood and shook her hand. "If you'd like I can go back and see if I have the title search," he said. "When the project folded, I kept all the files."

"That would be very helpful," she said, reaching into her purse and pulling out a card. "Here's my card. If you find anything, just call me and I'll come over."

"I'll do that," he said. "Have a good day, Miss O'Reilly."

"Mary," she said with a smile. "Please call me, Mary. And you have a good day too."

Chapter Nineteen

Bradley and Clarissa were already in the waiting room when Mary arrived. "Hi," she said, placing a quick kiss on each of their cheeks. "How did your day go?"

"Mine was great," Clarissa offered. "I got an A on my spelling test and we played kickball in gym."

"Congratulations," Mary replied with a smile. "That's great."

"Um, the Mayor gave me a gold star," Bradley inserted. "Am I great too?"

Clarissa and Mary laughed. "Oh, Daddy, you're always great," Clarissa said. "But did he really give you a gold star?"

Bradley sighed and then shook his head. "No, he didn't," he confessed. "I just thought it sounded good."

Mary leaned over and gave him another kiss. "It did sound good, darling," she said, winking in Clarissa's direction, "Just not as good as Clarissa."

Clarissa snorted and clapped a hand over her mouth to keep the giggles in. Bradley turned towards her, his eyebrows raised. "Oh, so you think that's funny, do you?"

"No Daddy," she choked, her hand still over her mouth. "I don't think it's funny."

"Good," he replied with a satisfied nod.

"I think it's hee- sterical," she added with a chorus of giggles.

Mary laughed. "That was brilliant, Clarissa," she said.

The inner office door opened and the laughter stopped immediately. All eyes went to the professional looking woman standing in the doorway. Her brown hair was pulled back in an efficient French twist, her business suit was navy blue and her tailored blouse was a crisp blue pinstripe. She looked down at the clipboard in her hand for a moment and then looked up again at the three of them. "The Alden family?" she asked.

"Yes, that's us," Bradley said.

She nodded and added a wisp of a smile. "Please, come in, all of you," she said, motioning into her office.

All three Aldens stood at the same time, like a choreographed marching band, and walked into her office, pausing in front of the long couch against the wall.

"Please sit," Dr. Springler commanded politely and all three Aldens sat, Bradley and Mary on either side of Clarissa.

Dr. Springler sat across from them on a leather office chair, her pen poised on the yellow pad on the clipboard and nodded. "Now, why don't you tell me why you're here today and what you'd like to get out of our meetings together?"

Clarissa's eyes widened and Mary could see the panic in them. "Why don't I start," Mary suggested, "since I was the one who set up the appointment."

Dr. Springler nodded for Mary to continue.

"We are an unusual family," Mary said. "Clarissa is Bradley's natural daughter, but she was lost to him for eight years and they finally found each other. Clarissa has been through all kinds of challenging situations in her young life - the loss of both her adoptive parents, a threat on her life and now, helping us figure out how to become a family. Bradley and I were recently married and we are figuring out how to be a couple, but also how to be parents. We both love Clarissa, but we understand that she has gone through a lot and needs time to learn how to trust us."

Dr. Springler looked at Clarissa. "What do you think about what your mother just said?" she asked. "Do you consider her your mother?"

Clarissa looked at Mary before responding to the doctor. Mary smiled at her. "Tell her what you really feel," she encouraged. "You're not going to hurt my feelings. I want you to be able to tell the truth."

Dr. Springler turned from Clarissa to Mary. "Actually, she might hurt your feelings," she said. "She should still tell the truth, but Clarissa needs to understand that you have feelings too. Feelings that can get hurt when someone is thoughtless."

Clarissa nodded and took a deep breath. "I had a first mom, I never knew her because she died when I was born, but Maggie told me about her. And then I had another mom, she adopted me, and she died too."

"Do you think all of your moms are going to die?" the doctor asked.

At first Clarissa just looked at the doctor, then a single tear slipped down her cheek and she finally nodded quickly. "Yes," she whispered. "I think moms die."

"How about dads," Dr. Springler asked. "Do dads die?"

Clarissa shook her head. "No, not like moms," she said. "Daddy Bradley has been looking for me since I was a baby. He never stopped and he didn't die. My moms get sick and die, bad guys don't get them."

130

"Ah, well that does make a difference, doesn't it," Dr. Springler said. "Are you worried about Mary getting sick?"

Clarissa glanced at Mary and then back at the doctor. "I heard her throwing up, in the morning," she said, her voice quivering. "My adopted mom threw up every day. She would run to the bathroom at night and turn on the water, she thought I couldn't hear her or I didn't know, but I did. She never talked to me about being sick, but I knew she was sick. I tried to help her. I got her water and food; I made her take her medicine. I was really quiet so she could sleep. I never told her about stuff that would worry her. But she still died anyway."

Dr. Springler turned to Mary. "Did you throw up this morning?" she asked.

Bradley and Mary's eyes met, Mary's brimming with tears in sympathy for the little girl. Turning in her seat, she took Clarissa's hands in her own. "Clarissa, you are right," she said. "I did throw up this morning. And I threw up yesterday morning too. And I think I threw up at my office this afternoon."

Clarissa eyes widened and she inhaled sharply, releasing the air in a stuttered shudder.

"But, the reason I am throwing up is because there is a baby growing inside me," she said. "And that often causes women to throw up."

131

Clarissa face turned from fear to wonder. "A baby?" she asked softly.

Mary nodded and placed her hand on Clarissa's cheek. "A baby brother or baby sister for you," she said. "How do you feel about being a big sister?"

Her bright and eager smile erased all doubts in Mary's mind. And when Clarissa wrapped her arms around Mary's waist and hugged her, Mary felt her heart melt with gratitude and love. She kissed the top of Clarissa's head. "You will be such a wonderful big sister," she said.

Clarissa looked up at her. "Will the baby call you mom?" she asked.

Mary nodded. "Yes, I think so."

"Then I'll call you mom too," she replied, and then nestled back into Mary's arms.

"Clarissa, that is a good decision," Dr. Springler said. "But are you still worried about Mary?"

Slipping out of Mary's arms, she sat back in her seat, thought about the doctor's question for a moment and nodded.

"Are you worried about Mary or are you worried that you are going to be left alone again?" the doctor asked.

Clarissa clasped her hands together tightly and avoided looking at Bradley and Mary and nodded again.

"You're worried that you are going to be left alone?" the doctor urged.

"What if they don't want me anymore?" Clarissa whispered, terrified at speaking the words aloud.

"That's a very scary thing to consider," the doctor replied. "And it's very brave of you to say it out loud."

She turned to Bradley. "How long did you search for your daughter?" she asked.

Bradley immediately remembered the day he and Jeannine were in the doctor's office looking at the tiny figure on the ultrasound screen. He knew he had fallen in love with his daughter at that moment. "Since before she was born," he said. "I never stopped looking for her."

"Are there things you did that would prove to her you never stopped looking? That you always wanted her?" she asked.

"He painted the room pink," Mary whispered, remembering the anguished joy in Jeanine's voice when she realized Bradley had still painted the nursery as they had planned.

"Pardon me?" Dr. Springler asked.

Bradley turned to Clarissa. "Just before your mother was taken by the bad man, we went to the doctor and had an ultrasound. That's a special machine that lets the doctors see how the baby is doing inside the mother. During that ultrasound, we saw that you were a little girl. I was so thrilled that I was going to be your father. On the way home, I insisted we stop at the hardware store and buy pink paint for your bedroom. Your mom thought I was pretty silly, because we had just painted your room white. But, I wanted my little girl to have a pink room. Then, your mom was taken. I searched for her and for you. I followed every lead and went all over the country looking for you. But when I didn't have any leads and when I was just waiting for people to call me, I wanted to make sure that when I found you, you would have the perfect room. So, I painted your bedroom pink."

She looked over at him. "You painted my room at Mary's pink too," she said.

He nodded, taking a moment to gather his emotions before he spoke. "I always wanted you to have a pink bedroom," he said. "It just took longer than I thought it would."

"How does that make you feel, Clarissa?" Dr. Springler asked.

"Not so afraid," she said.

"That's great," she replied. "That's all I want to do for today. But you all have homework. I want you to each take one of these notebooks and I want you to write down your feelings about your family, not just happy ones, but also angry ones or sad ones. Be very honest. Can you do that?"

The three nodded their heads and picked up notebooks.

"When would you like to see us again?" Mary asked.

"Well, I'd like to see Clarissa next week," she said. "But in the meantime, if there are any major issues or problems, feel free to call me."

"We will," Bradley said. "Thank you."

She handed Clarissa one of her cards. "And this is just for you," she said. "If you ever feel really sad or angry, I want you to call me. Okay?"

Clarissa nodded and smiled. "Okay, I will. I promise."

Chapter Twenty

Mary sat on the couch; her feet curled up beneath her, a cup of tea next to her and pulled out her laptop. She glanced up to watch Bradley come down the stairs. "Is she asleep?" she asked.

He nodded. "Yeah, after you left I only had to read one more chapter until she was fast asleep," he said, sitting on the couch next to her and pulling her into his arms. "How are you feeling?"

She leaned back and snuggled against him. "I'm a little tired, but overall I feel good," she said. "Today was a good day."

"Well, good after you could escape the house from the fumes of the noxious peppers and onions," he teased, kissing the side of her neck.

"Don't remind me," she chuckled. "But dinner was amazing."

"Yeah, it was pretty amazing, if I do say so myself," he boasted. "It's amazing what these hands can do. Pick up a phone, dial a number and then drive to Imperial Palace for take-out."

Laughing softly, she felt herself relax against him. "Well, I've been craving sweet and sour chicken," she admitted. "So, you were my hero."

"It's so easy to be your hero," he said, reading over her shoulder at the notes on the screen. "Now, tell me about the case you're working on, if that will be helpful."

"Actually, yes, it would be great just to get things straight in my mind," she said. "Dale Johnson; a really nice man, great family, hardworking, salt of the earth type. He winds up dead at the bottom of a grain bin. The family decides to treat it like a farm accident —that's what they tell the Sheriff's Office."

"So, no investigation, nothing criminal?" he asked.

"Right, no law enforcement brought in," she replied. "Just one of those things. But, it seems that in the back of their minds everyone is suspicious of everyone else. No one believes that Dale would close himself inside a silo. No one believes that it's merely coincidental that his death occurs just when it would be advantageous for them to sell the property. A sale that he was against."

"So you have motive for murder," he said, as he lifted his hands and massaged her shoulders.

She purred softly. "That feels so good, but it's really not helping me concentrate."

He chuckled into her ear. "Just relax and let the thoughts flow freely."

"Okay, but wake me when I start to snore," she replied. "So motive. The banker whose job was on the line and was dating the daughter said the sale was the keystone to the whole project."

"So the banker is a suspect. He had motive and opportunity."

"Yes, he did," Mary said. "But he was awfully upfront and offended by Jessie's suspicions. She's the daughter he dated. They broke up after her father's death because she either felt he had something to do with the death or she just didn't like the way his company took advantage of the circumstances."

"But they couldn't have just taken the property. The family had to agree to it."

"Exactly," Mary said, sitting up and turning to face Bradley. "And Josh, the oldest son, was the driving force behind the sale. Quinn, the banker, told me that the incentives offered by Maughold were running out and they were offered close to ten times more than the property was worth."

"That's a lot of money for farmland."

"Yeah, it is," Mary agreed. "I don't know why they were offered so much. Maybe they had the water access or the road access, but whatever it was, the Johnson farm was vital to the whole project."

"So Josh sold the land soon after his dad died."

"And then the project died. So they got paid a fortune for plain old farmland."

"Do you know how much land was included in the deal?"

Mary leaned back against Bradley again and closed her eyes for a moment, trying to visualize the sales contract she had reviewed that morning. "I think it was 500 acres. Does that sound right?"

He nodded. "Yeah, the average farm in the area is close to 400 acres, so that's right in the neighborhood."

"And the appraised value for the land was $2500 an acre," she said. "But, from what Quinn said, the incentive would increase that more than ten times."

"So, you're going from about $1.25 million to $12.5 million," he said. "More than a ten million dollar difference."

"Okay, first, I'm impressed that you could do that in your head," she said, turning to face him. "So, you are in charge of helping Clarissa with math. Second, ten million dollars is a lot of motive."

"What's your next step?"

"I want to meet with the children and see what they say," she said. "It sounds like suspicion has really pulled the family apart."

"I can't believe they let a little money destroy our family," Dale said as he appeared in front of them in the middle of the living room.

Mary reached over and touched Bradley's hand. "Can you see him?" she asked, wondering what Bradley would think of Dale's broken and twisted body.

Bradley nodded. "Yeah, not a nice way to die," he whispered.

"Ten million dollars," Dale scoffed. "It don't mean nothing if you don't have family. Do you really think my kids killed me for ten million dollars?"

"I don't know yet," she said. "I do know that the land was sold and a lot of money was made. I know that although there was never an investigation, there is a lot of suspicion. They are protecting each other, but not trusting each other."

"I thought I taught them to be better than this," he said. "I thought I raised them to be honest and loyal."

"Well, they have the loyalty part down," Bradley said. "In fifteen years they haven't betrayed each other."

"You can see me?" Dale asked, surprised by Bradley's comment.

"Yes, when he and I touch, he can see ghosts too," Mary answered. "Dale, this is my husband, Bradley. Bradley, this is Dale Johnson, the ghost I was telling you about."

Glancing down at his wife, Bradley smiled. She had no idea how odd that sentence was, and yet, for her it was as common as introducing a next door neighbor. He looked up and met Dale's eyes and felt a mutual understanding pass between them.

"Not every day your wife introduces you to a dead person in your living room," he said.

"Oh, you'd be surprised," Bradley answered with a grin. "Life with Mary is anything but boring."

"But worth every minute, I'd guess," Dale said.

Bradley nodded. "Oh, yes, every minute," he replied. "So, Dale, are there any other people, other than your immediate family who could have murdered you?"

Dale ran his fingers down his broken and narrowed chin. "Well, now, I haven't given that much thought," he said. "This whole idea of being dead and murdered is fairly new to me."

"That's a good point, Bradley," Mary said. "Are there any other people who benefited?"

"Well, the obvious one is Maughold, but I don't think they'd send a hit man out to do me in just because I wouldn't sell my property," Dale said. "There were plenty of other farms just as big as mine that would have worked for them."

"But Quinn said your place was the keystone farm," Mary said. "Without your farm the whole deal was dead."

Pausing and staring at Mary for a moment, Dale shook his head. "That doesn't make sense at all," he said. "My farm was no different than the farms across the road. I never heard anything about being a keystone property."

"According to Quinn, Josh got ten times what the property was worth," Mary said.

"Ten times," Dale exclaimed. "Why in the hell would they do that? There's something not right here. They didn't find oil or gold underneath my land, did they?"

"No, the project got voted down, so your land is just sitting there," Mary said.

"Sitting there?" Dale cried even louder. "Like set aside? No crops, no plowing, nothing?"

"As far as I know, nothing," Mary replied.

"My dad and granddad would be rolling in their graves if they knew their land was just barren and wasted," Dale said, shaking his head. "You need to find out the story and you need to get someone farming my land."

"I'll do my best," Mary promised.

"Well, you do that, but take care you don't do too much and hurt that little bundle you're carrying," he replied.

"You know?" Bradley asked, looking at Dale and then he turned to Mary. "He knows?"

Mary nodded. "Well, he witnessed me not at my best," she said.

"She was puking like a geyser," Dale added, with a kind smile. "Same thing happened to my Greta every time she was pregnant."

"Dale was nice enough to point me in the direction of the bathroom."

"Seemed like the smart thing to do at the time," he said. "The carpeting looked new."

Bradley choked and then grinned. "Well, thank you for helping her."

"No problem and congratulations, young man," Dale replied and then, as he started to fade away, looked at Mary. "Thank you for all you're doing."

"My pleasure," Mary said, as she watched Dale disappear.

Leaning back in Bradley's arms, she sighed. "He seems like such a nice man," she said sadly. "How could anyone kill him?"

Bradley wrapped his arms around her and kissed the top of her head. "I have no doubt that you will be the one to figure that out."

Chapter Twenty-one

The prestigious accounting firm was housed in the historic Lincoln-Douglas Building on the corner of Galena Avenue and Exchange Street. Mary walked up the stone steps of the 1890s Italian Renaissance style building with its partial ionic columns flanking the doorway and pushed open the door. The tiled entryway had been remodeled to reflect the building's illustrious history and immediately brought you back to a different era when Freeport had been a bustling insurance capital. Pressing the worn black button to summon the vintage elevator, Mary hoped that only the façade was vintage and that the mechanics were updated and working smoothly.

The elevator slid smoothly to a stop on the second floor and Mary stepped out, walking the few yards to the door advertising the accounting firm. Pushing the heavy wooden door open, she stepped inside an office space with polished wood floors, built-in oak bookcases and Oriental rugs on the floor.

The accounting business must be doing well, she thought as she walked over to the oak reception desk. "Hi, I have an appointment with Jessie Johnson," Mary informed the young woman behind the desk.

"Just a moment, I'll let her know you're here," the woman replied with a pleasant smile. "Your name please?"

"Mary Alden."

"Please have a seat, Ms. Alden," she replied. "I'm sure Jessie will be out momentarily."

Mary walked over to the small waiting area, examining the magazines on the desk, *Money, Fortune, Journal of Accountancy* and *Martha Stewart,* and smiled —they certainly had an eclectic customer base. Looking beyond the waiting area into the long hallway that housed the offices, Mary noticed a quick flash of shadow. Watching carefully, she saw it again. The ghost of a diminutive man with large, heavy glasses and a dark suit jacket whisked back and forth through the walls of the office. He had a pencil stuck behind his ear and he seemed to be frantically searching for something. He stopped in the middle of the hall and stared at Mary. She glanced at the receptionist, who was busy with her computer and then turned back to the ghost. As inconspicuously as she could, she pulled her hair back over her ear and nodded pointedly. The ghost reached up and retrieved the pencil. With a wide smile and a wink, he bowed to Mary and then faded from sight.

Been there, done that, Mary thought.

"Ms. Alden?"

Mary jumped a little and turned to see a fairly young woman standing behind her. "Sorry, you startled me," Mary said. "I guess I expected you to come from that direction." She pointed towards the long hallway she'd been watching.

"Oh, that's for the senior accountants," she said with a smile and then she added with a whisper, "I've heard once they make it to the long hall, they never leave."

Mary chuckled. "You just never know about those things."

"I booked the small conference room for our meeting," she said, leading Mary down an adjacent hall. "I'm so sorry about the lien. I can't imagine what that's for."

She opened the door to a small room that held a table and six chairs. In the corner was a smaller table that held a phone and a coffee maker. "Would you care for anything to drink?" she asked Mary.

"Oh, no, I'm fine," Mary said, taking a seat and waiting for Jessie to sit before she began so she could watch her expression. "Actually, I've been doing a little investigation of my own about the lien. I thought it might be helpful."

"Oh? Who did you meet with?" Jessie asked.

"Quinn. Quinn Edmonson," Mary replied, watching Jessie's face. "He was very helpful."

Mary was not surprised to see the same emotions wash over Jessie's face that she had seen the day before on Quinn's. But this time, the one that lasted the longest was regret.

"So, how's he doing?" Jessie asked. "Quinn."

"Well, I just met with him for a few minutes, but he seems to be doing well," Mary replied. "He remembered your property immediately. He told me that he really liked your family and made a…a personal connection."

Jessie nodded. "Yes, we became quite close to Quinn when he was representing Maughold."

"What happened?" Mary asked. "I mean, if you don't mind me asking. He seems like such a nice man."

Jessie stared past Mary for a moment, gathering her thoughts. "My father passed away, suddenly," she said. "And the family was pretty torn up about it."

"Not torn up enough to keep the land in the family," Dale muttered as he appeared in the room next to Jessie.

Jessie shivered and rubbed her arms with her hands. "I'm sorry, it's suddenly cold in here," she said. "Are you comfortable?"

148

"Yes, I'm fine," she said, pleased to know that Jessie was sensitive to paranormal visitors. It might end up being very helpful. "You mentioned your father passed away. Had he been sick?"

She smiled sadly. "No, my dad was never sick a day in his life," she said. "He always said he didn't have time to be sick and, really, I think the germs obeyed him." She sighed softly. "Everyone obeyed Dad."

"Sure, just ask her about the time she used my razor to shave her legs," Dale grumbled. "Nearly destroyed my face the next day."

Mary smiled to herself. "So, he sounds like he was pretty stern."

"Oh, no, he just grumbled a lot," she said. "He had a soft heart and would do anything for anyone. He was the one who stayed up all night with a sick calf; he was the one who rescued the barn kittens when their mothers abandoned them. He was the one who sat up and waited for me to get home from my dates when I was in high school." Her voice broke and she brushed away a tear. "He was a great dad."

"It was easy when you have a great daughter," Dale said, his voice thick with emotion.

"So how did he die?" Mary asked.

"Well, everyone said it was a farming accident," she replied. "But it was really hard to believe. Dad was never careless. He taught us to practice safety rules all the time. He told us that farming was one of the most dangerous occupations you could have, but mostly because people got careless. I just don't believe he closed himself into a grain silo."

"What did the police say?" Mary asked, knowing the answer.

"There was no investigation," Jessie said. "I guess we decided it was better to be thought of as an accident."

"Better?"

Jessie shook her head. "I'm sorry; you don't need to hear our family's history. You're here about the lien. So, what do you need from us?"

"I need your signature and the signatures of the rest of your family stating that you will be responsible for the lien," Mary said. "I know the original contractor is dead, but you can never tell if someone from his estate would try to pursue this. If, as your mother said, it's just a mistake, then it's no big deal. But, just in case, I'd like to have all my bases covered."

"Well, of course," Jessie said. "I can sign it and then I can have Josh and Abe sign it too."

Mary opened her briefcase and took out the fake document. "I hate to be a bother, but my lawyer said that I needed to be present when it's signed," she said. "So no one can claim they never saw it."

Reaching across the desk, Jessie picked up the paper, skimmed the contents and quickly signed the bottom.

"She writes like her mother," Dale said, looking over Jessie's shoulder.

Jessie looked up instantly. "Did you say something?" she asked.

Mary shook her head. "No. What did you hear?"

Shaking her head, she smiled sadly. "It's funny how your mind plays games with you," she said. "I thought I heard my dad."

"I've had that happen to me," Mary said. "And sometimes I feel like maybe there's a message in it for me."

Meeting Mary's eyes, Jessie paused. "A message?"

Mary nodded. "Well, it's worked for me," she said. "Who knows, your dad might be trying to help us get the house sold."

"No, he wouldn't be helping with that," she said decidedly. "Dad wanted the house and the land to stay in the family. That was his greatest wish."

"Oh," Mary replied. "Then, can I ask, why you are selling it?"

"I can't walk through the house without thinking about him," she said. "And, you'll probably think I'm crazy, but sometimes I think I actually see him or hear him."

"Are you saying your house is haunted?" Mary asked, a teasing tone in her voice.

"Only by my memories," Jessie said.

Chapter Twenty-two

Dale appeared next to Mary once the elevator doors closed. "She could hear me," he said. "How do you explain that?"

"Love," Mary said simply. "She misses you and part of her yearns for any contact she can make with you."

"Sometimes you take your children's love for granted," he muttered. "Sometimes you don't realize what your absence will do to them."

"It sounds like you were a great dad," Mary said. "And that Jessie knew she was loved. You can't do better than that."

He sighed deeply. "I don't think Jessie had anything to do with my death."

"Well, I'm inclined to agree with you," she said. "But until I have all the facts, I don't want to jump to any conclusions."

The elevator stopped and as the door slid open, Dale faded away. Hurrying across the lobby, Mary stepped out into the bright, late spring day. The air smelled fresh and the Freeport Downtown Development Foundation had planted flowers in the planters throughout downtown, so everything looked a little brighter. Looking at her watch, she decided she still had time to meet with Abe at the repair shop.

She crossed the street and walked the two blocks to the auto repair shop. Pushing open the glass door, she walked to the service desk and waited. A tall young man who immediately reminded her of Dale came walking in from the garage area, wiping his hands on a shop towel.

"Can I help you?" he asked.

Mary studied him for a moment. She had never seen a person so devoid of emotion, like he was just empty inside. "Hi," she finally said with a smile. "I'm looking for Abe Johnson."

Cocking his head, it was his turn to study her for a moment. "I'm Abe," he said. "And I'm not interested."

"Not interested?" Mary asked.

"Not interested in whatever it is you're selling."

"Really? Do I look like a salesperson?" Mary replied with a grin, looking down at her outfit. "Do I at least look like a successful salesperson?"

"Listen lady," he began impatiently.

"Mary. Mary Alden," she said. "And I'm here about the house you and your family are selling."

He was instantly taken aback. "I'm sorry," he said. "But my sister is handling that. Her name is Jessie…"

"I've already met with Jessie," Mary replied. "And now I need to meet with you. There's a lien on the deed and I need your signature stating that you, and the rest of your family, will be responsible for any obligation incurred if the lien is optioned."

"A lien. What the hell?"

"It seems that a contractor who did some work on the house years ago placed a lien on it, until the work was paid for," she said.

"The work was paid for," Abe said forcefully. "My dad paid all his debts. On time and in full. My dad didn't believe in credit. I know it was paid for."

"He sure has a lot of confidence in me," Dale said softly in Mary's ear.

"Your dad's payment isn't in question," Mary said. "Through some error, the lien was never taken off the property. The contractor is no longer alive, or I'd go to him. But, in case his estate decides to try and come after the property, which they probably won't, I need your family to agree to be responsible for the obligation."

"And if I don't sign?" he asked.

"Don't be an ass, boy," Dale criticized. "She hasn't done anything to you."

Mary shrugged. "Then I don't buy the house," she said. "And more than likely, no one else will buy it either."

Abe took a deep breath. "I apologize," he said contritely. "You haven't done anything to me; I'm just a little sensitive when it comes to the house."

"I understand your dad died at the house," Mary replied sympathetically.

"Yeah, but what you don't understand is that I killed him."

"What?" Dale yelled in Mary's ear.

Trying not to react to Dale's outburst, Mary took a deep breath and met Abe's eyes. "I understand it was a farming accident," she said. "How could you be responsible?"

He tossed the rag down on the counter and ran his hand impatiently through his hair. "One of the first rules of farming, one of the first things Dad ever taught me was to check and double check," he said. "I should have checked the grain silo before I emptied the truckload into the silo. I should have opened it up and gone inside. If I had done that, he wouldn't have died."

Dale snorted. "Abe was the most diligent of the three, I can't believe he didn't check it."

"So, you didn't check the silo at all?" Mary asked.

"Well sure I did," he replied. "Before I went out to the field I checked it. Looked it over and then latched the door good and tight."

"Then why the hell is he blaming himself?" Dale shouted.

"You checked it once and everything was fine?" Mary asked again.

"I said it was," Abe replied.

"Would there be any reason to check it again?" she asked.

He shrugged. "Not normally, but if I had…"

"Did you ever think you were set up?" Mary asked impatiently.

"What?"

"You're so busy blaming yourself that you never stopped to figure out why your dad would have gone into the silo and locked the door behind himself?"

"He wouldn't have done that," he said. "He knew better."

"So, if you checked earlier and your dad wouldn't have done it himself," Mary explained. "Then someone put your dad in there and locked him in, knowing you already checked."

Abe staggered back against the wall, his eyes wide and his face white. "Someone murdered my dad," he said and then he turned to Mary. "Why didn't someone investigate his death?"

Mary met his eyes. "Because everyone in your family thinks they are protecting someone else in the family."

He suddenly clapped his mouth shut and he was silent for a few moments. "I got no more to say to you," he finally said. "I'll sign your paper, but then you and your crazy ideas need to stay the hell away from my family."

"He thinks it's Josh," Dale said. "He's protecting Josh."

Mary handed Abe the paper and he scrawled out his signature. "Thank you, Abe," she said.

"I better not hear that you're spreading rumors about members of my family," he threatened. "I'll sue you. I haven't touched a penny of the money we got when we sold the land, but I'll use it all to protect my family."

"Don't worry, Abe," she said. "I'm not out to hurt your family."

158

Mary turned and left the store; she was a little shaken by Abe's vehemence.

"I never taught him to treat a lady like that," Dale said. "But I can't say I wasn't a little bit proud when he stood up for family like that."

Mary inhaled deeply and nodded. "Yeah, even if he thinks Josh did it, he'd fight for him," she said.

"He's a good brother," Dale said.

"And a good son," Mary added.

"Yeah, a good son…a great son," Dale said and then he faded away.

Chapter Twenty-three

The phone rang as Mary entered her office and she hurried to answer it. "Mary O'Reilly," she said, holding the phone between her chin and shoulder as she put her briefcase down and pulled out her laptop.

"Girl, when are you going to remember you're married?" Gracie Williams teased on the other end of the phone.

"Gracie," Mary said with a smile. "Thanks for reminding me. I was wondered what he was doing sleeping in my bed."

"Honey, when a man looks that fine I sure hope he's doing more than just sleeping in your bed."

Mary blushed. "Gracie," she replied with shock in her voice. "Of course he is. He's stealing the blankets, taking up my side of the bed and snoring. Is that what you mean?"

Gracie chuckled. "Well of course that's what I mean," she said. "This is during working hours, we wouldn't want to talk about anything scandalous."

"Oh, and it would be scandalous," Mary assured her.

"So, since we can't talk about it, why don't you tell me how your conversation about the baby went?"

Mary sighed softly. "It was so great," she said. "Well, once we figured out that I wasn't dying and Bradley wasn't leaving me. But after that, it was great."

"I'm not going to even ask what all that in between stuff was, but he's happy about the baby?"

"He's thrilled and he's trying so hard to take care of me," Mary said. "Yesterday morning he got up early to make me my favorite breakfast- burritos with green peppers and onions."

"No he didn't," she replied. "Did you puke right there in the kitchen or did you make it to the bathroom?"

"Actually, I smelled the green peppers and onions when I was still upstairs, so I got to take care of it in the privacy of the master bathroom," she said with a laugh. "And once he realized how it affected me, he got me a tea to go and some soda crackers."

"He's a good man," Gracie said. "And now, how did your meeting with the child psychologist go?"

Mary sat back in her chair and pondered for a moment. "You know, she wasn't as warm and fuzzy as I thought she would be," she said. "I mean, she

161

seemed competent and professional, but for some reason I thought she would be more approachable. Especially since she is working with children."

"Well, sometimes being a little distant can be helpful," Gracie said. "She's not their friend, but she is there to help them. An authority figure, like a teacher."

"I suppose that might work," Mary said. "We had some good conversations yesterday and really had some important breakthroughs. So, you might be right."

"But?" Gracie asked with humor in her voice.

Mary chuckled. "You know me so well," she said. "But, she just didn't seem happy."

"Mary, your responsibilities do not include making everyone around you happy," she said. "Sometimes people just need to work things out."

"You're right…"

"Of course I'm right," Gracie interrupted. "That was never in question."

Mary laughed out loud. "Gracie, I miss you," she said.

"When are you coming to Chicago?" Gracie asked. "We need to do lunch so you can enlighten me on your scandalous life."

"Soon, I'll be coming soon," she said. "I thought I'd wait until I'm past my first trimester to tell my family about the baby. So, we'll probably be coming in next month."

"Well, you just tell me when and we'll schedule a long lunch," Gracie said. "And maybe by then you'll have a little meat on your skinny self."

Mary eyed the bag containing the corned beef sandwich and large deli pickle now sitting on her desk. "Well, if I keep satisfying my cravings, I'll have more than meat," she said. "I'll have fat."

"As long as you're eating healthy and limiting your sweets, you're just fine," Gracie said. "And I'm a doctor."

"You're a psychologist, that doesn't count," Mary countered.

"Honey, when you want an excuse to eat chocolate, who are you going to listen to?" Gracie asked.

"Now that you mention it, I've always thought that you were much smarter than any other doctor I've seen."

"Now you're talking," Gracie replied with a laugh. "Well, I gotta run now. You take care, here? And call me if you need anything."

"I will," Mary said. "Take care, Gracie."

Chapter Twenty-four

After finishing her lunch and making a few phone calls, Mary found that she had a couple of hours before she could do anything more on the Johnson case. But ever since Gracie had mentioned chocolate, Mary couldn't keep her mind off of the dark chocolate ice cream at Union Dairy. Of course, she couldn't go there unless she had at least started her investigation about Erika.

"Okay, library first," she said aloud. "And the fact that it is right next door to Union Dairy is just a coincidence."

The public library was nearly empty, but since it was the middle of the day during a school and work day, Mary wasn't surprised. She walked up the curving steps to the second floor and headed to the local history section. One entire section of shelving held copies of the Polaris, the yearbook of Freeport High School. The first copy was dated 1905 and the library had copies of most years since then. By the kind of clothing she was wearing and her hairstyle, Mary estimated that Erika was in school in the fifties. But the song she chose, The Everly's Brothers' *All I Have to Do Is Dream,* was released in 1958, so Mary picked up the 1958 Polaris first. Flipping through the yearbook she smiled at the bouffant hairstyles and cat-eye glasses so common during that era. They boys had slicked back "flat tops" or crew cuts and the girls looked like carbon-copies of Sandra Dee or Elizabeth Taylor. She also noted that the boys all wore suits and ties for their class photos and most of the girls wore starched white embroidered collars over buttoned up sweaters. She studied the names underneath each photo, but no "Erika" was listed so she flipped over to the section that had the class photos.

Instead of individual pictures, like the Seniors, the Juniors had a large group photo. The Junior Class photo was shot in the gym, with students lined up on bleachers so everyone could be seen. There were only two hundred students in the Junior Class, so eight rows of twenty-five were assembled on the bleachers. Mary studied the photo for a moment when something at the very top of the group caught her eye. She pulled the book closer and studied the black and white photo. There on the very top, a level above the final row, the face of the young girl peeked out between the heads of several very tall boys.

Mary placed a piece of paper between the pages, closed the book and walked out from between the shelves. A librarian was sitting behind a desk next to the local history area.

"Hi," Mary said as she approached the woman. "I was wondering if you might happen to have a magnifying glass."

"Looking at old photos are you?" the librarian asked with a smile as she slid out a desk drawer and reached in for a large black-rimmed magnifying glass.

"Yes, I am," Mary said. "But it's hard to see some of the details."

The woman handed her the glass. "You might want to go over there by the microfiche machine," she suggested. "The light is much stronger over there."

Thanking her, Mary made her way to an empty table next to the microfiche machine and opened the book to the Junior Class photo. Using the glass, she leaned over and studied the face in the photo; it looked like Erika, the ghost at Union Dairy Ice Cream Shop. But as she looked closer, she realized there was something very odd about her face. Not only was she above the rest of the group, but when you looked close enough, you could see the row of bleachers through her face.

Mary slowly sat up, still staring at the book. That was a photo of a ghost. Erika had died before her Junior Class photo shoot and her ghost took her place.

"I wonder how many other people realized she was in the yearbook," Mary wondered. "She's not really hidden at all."

Picking the book up again, she scanned the caption of names, at the very end of the list was a note. *Deceased: Erika Arnold*

"Well, at least I know who she is," Mary whispered. "Now all I have to do is find out how she died and why she's still hanging around."

Chapter Twenty-five

Mary entered Union Dairy armed with a healthy craving for dark chocolate and some more information on Erika. It was the middle of the afternoon and school was in session, so the restaurant was nearly empty. She walked over to the counter and was greeted by a college-aged girl.

"Hi, what can I get you?" she asked.

"Dark chocolate," Mary said.

"Okay, we have dark chocolate with pieces of coconut candy bars, dark chocolate with pieces of brownie, dark chocolate with bits of semi-sweet dark chocolate chips and dark chocolate with chocolate-covered raspberries. Which one would you like?"

"You're kidding me, right?" Mary asked. "I have to choose?"

The girl smiled and shook her head. "No, actually, I can put a scoop of each into these small cardboard containers that fit perfectly into your freezer. Then you can try them all and not feel like you are overdoing it."

Mary looked at the small six ounce containers and quickly calculated how many could fit in the small freezer section of her office refrigerator.

"Okay, I'll take three containers of each," she said with a smile.

"You want twelve in all?" the girl asked, trying to hide her astonishment.

Mary nodded. "Yes, twelve in all," she answered.

The girl looked over to the stack of containers. "We're down to our last five," she said. "I need to run back to the storeroom for the rest. I'll be back in a minute."

"Take your time," Mary replied.

"You should have asked for a taste of them," a small voice next to her said.

Mary turned and looked down at Brandon.

"Hi," she said. "That's a great idea; I'll have to use it next time."

"My mom and I used to get tastes all the time," he said. "We would have a contest to see the best taste combination."

"What was the best?" Mary asked.

"I liked the bubble gum, cookie dough and Rocky Road taste," he said. "Mom liked the chocolate, cheesecake and strawberry taste."

"Oh, I'm going to have to go with your mom's choice," she said.

Brandon glanced around. "Have you found her yet?" he asked. "I'm still looking."

Mary took a quick breath as tears stung her eyes. "No, I'm sorry, Brandon, I haven't," she said. "Maybe you could give me some clues that would help me out."

"Clues?" he asked with a wide smile. "Like in Blue's Clues?" Naming the popular children's show.

"Just like that," Mary said, glancing around just to be sure they were still alone.

"Okay," Brandon said. "Let me think."

She smiled to herself as she watched the little boy screw up his face in concentration. Finally he looked up with a smile. "I kind of remember a big building," he said. "We went there a lot. And after, we would come here."

"A big building?" Mary asked. "Like a church or the library?"

"No," he said, shaking his head and chewing his lower lip as he thought. "They listened to my heart and tapped my knee with a hammer."

"The hospital?" Mary asked. "You used to go with your mom to the hospital."

"Yes," he said. "You got the clue. Now you can find my mom."

Mary heard the returning footsteps of the waitress. "Okay, Brandon, I'll keep looking and let you know."

"Thanks," he said with a brilliant smile. "Thanks a lot."

Chapter Twenty-six

Josh Johnson's office was in the Stewart Centre building on Douglas Street. The building was the only high-rise in Freeport and with a total of twelve floors; it stood well above the other structures in the downtown. Mary took the elevator up to the seventh floor and stepped out onto the carpeted lobby. She scanned the small marque on the wall in front of the elevators and found that Johnson Enterprises was located in Suite 705. Turning up the hall, she quickly found the room and knocked on the door.

"Come in," a man's voice responded and Mary opened the door and let herself in.

Her jaw nearly dropped when the man behind the desk stood and greeted her. He looked just like Dale. But Dale not injured and in the flesh.

"Are you okay?" Josh asked, coming around his desk quickly when he saw the surprise on Mary's face.

She shook her head. "I'm so sorry," she said, slightly embarrassed by her reaction. "It's just that you look so much like your father, you surprised me."

"No one's compared me to my dad in years," he said softly, almost to himself.

172

After a quick moment, he regained his focus and smiled politely at her. "What can I do to help you?" he asked. "You said something about the house?"

Sitting down, Mary pulled the lien document from her briefcase and handed it to him. He reviewed it, crossing back around to the other side of his desk and sat down slowly.

"I'm surprised to see this," he said, still studying the paper. "I know the work was completed and paid for. Have you contacted Rogers Construction?"

"No, I didn't," she replied. "I didn't want to stir anything up for your family, not knowing the situation behind the lien. I did find out, though, that Steve Rogers has passed away."

Josh nodded. "Yeah, I went to his funeral," he said. "He and my dad were good friends. I thought he'd want me to be there."

"Hell, I wanted to be there," Dale said, appearing behind Josh. "But you went and killed me, so that kind of prevented it."

Josh glanced over his shoulder and then turned back to Mary. "Did you hear something?" he asked.

"Um, no," Mary lied. "No I didn't."

173

Josh shrugged and glanced back down at the document. "So what do you need from me?"

"I just need your signature," she said. "The document basically states that you and your family will be responsible for any debts or obligations set forth in the lien."

"Do you know how much the lien is for?" he asked.

"No, I didn't pull that paperwork," she said. "Once again, I didn't want to uncover anything that was best left alone. When I first saw the lien, I didn't know anything about your father, so I didn't know what to think."

Josh's head snapped up. "What do you mean by that?"

Once again, Mary tried to read emotions as she spoke. "I didn't know he was such an honest man," she said.

"He was a hard-ass," Josh replied. "A stubborn hard-ass. But, yes, he was honest."

"You don't seem to admire him as much as your siblings did," she said.

"Well, when you're the oldest, you get a different perspective," Josh said. "When you're the oldest, there are obligations that are assumed from the moment you're born. At least when you're the oldest in a multi-generational agricultural family."

"Ah, so your future was decided before you even had a say in the matter?" Mary asked.

"Course it was," Dale said. "That farm gave you the house you lived in and the food you ate. Nothing wrong with a legacy. Should have been grateful for the opportunity."

"Yeah, before I was ten my life was all set out before me," he said. "Dad would always say things like 'When Josh takes over the farm' or 'When you run the farm, you can do things your own way.'"

"What did you want to do?" Mary asked.

"What I'm doing now," he said. "I work the financial ends of things. I help other farmers invest their money, so they have a different kind of legacy for their kids. Not just back-breaking hard work and an uncertain future, I help them plan for a future."

"Nothing wrong with hard work," Dale muttered. "It was good enough for me, my dad and his dad before him."

"Is that why you wanted to sell the land right after your dad died?" she asked. "For the future?"

"Or for the money?" Dale spat.

"Is that what they told you?" Josh asked, standing and pacing behind his desk, nearly running through his father. "Is that what Jessie and Abe said?"

"Well, I don't think they used those exact words," she replied.

"Mr. Gartner told me I needed to sell in order to take advantage of the incentive," Josh said. "He told me if waited I would lose millions of dollars. I wasn't just thinking about myself, but of Jessie, Abe and Mom. It was a lot of money."

"That's a lie," Dale said, shaking his head slowly. "Gartner never sold his property. He was on the county board and they were the ones deciding on allowing the corporation to come in. It would have been a conflict of interest. He would have had to recuse himself from the voting."

"But your dad didn't want the land to be sold," Mary said.

"Yeah, but my dad wasn't around anymore to make any of those decisions," Josh said. "He wasn't going to run the farm and I sure wasn't going to be the sacrificial goat and run it."

"How about Abe?" Dale asked. "He could have done it."

"Wasn't Abe interested?" Mary asked.

"Abe," Josh closed his eyes and sighed. "Abe was so buried in guilt that he didn't leave his room for a week, except for the funeral. He blamed himself for dad's death."

"But it wasn't Abe's fault, was it?" Mary asked.

Josh shook his head. "No. It wasn't Abe fault," he said quietly.

Sitting down suddenly, he grabbed a pen and quickly signed the document. "Okay, you have my signature," he said, pushing the paper across the desk to her. "Now, please, get out of my office."

Chapter Twenty-seven

"I got your text, Mary," Rosie said as she entered Mary's office. "I can't believe you've already met with all of Dale's kids. So, what do you think? Did they kill their dad?"

Mary looked up and grinned. Rosie was still wearing the plastic shawl from the local beauty parlor and her head was covered with blocks of shiny foil.

"Rosie, what were you doing when you got my text?" she asked.

"Having my hair done," she replied, sliding into the seat in front of Mary's desk. "It has to process for twenty minutes anyway, so I figured I'd hurry down and talk to you."

"Really, Rosie, it could have waited," Mary chuckled.

"Well, I couldn't," she argued. "This is the very first time I've actually hired a ghost investigator. So, what's up?"

"All of the children were willing to sign the fake document about the lien," Mary replied. "But it seems that all of them are not convinced Dale's death was an accident."

"Why didn't they go to the police?"

"Because they think they're protecting each other," Mary said. "Even Greta was suspicious, but she never told anyone because she didn't want to get her children in trouble."

"So, who did it?" Rosie asked.

Mary shrugged. "I don't know yet," she said. "I'm sure it's linked with the sale of the land, but I still need a strong motive."

"They made a lot of money," Rosie said. "Isn't that a good motive?"

"Yes, money's a good motive," Mary said. "But does it outweigh the other variables?"

Sitting back in the chair and adjusting the shawl, so the back of the chair was protected, Rosie cocked her head slightly, sending all the foil slips shifting to one side. "What do you mean by outweighing other variables?"

"Okay, well, if someone offered you a million dollars to divorce Stanley, what would you say?"

Rosie pondered her response for a moment. "Could I marry him again, after I got the million?"

Mary laughed. "No, you could never see him again."

"Then no," Rosie said with a quick shrug. "I love Stanley more than a million dollars."

"And love is one of those variables you have to consider," Mary said. "If Dale's kids loved him, they wouldn't kill him for money."

"Did they love him?" Rosie asked.

"Yeah, did they love me?" Dale asked, appearing next to Rosie. He looked over at her and did a double-take. "What the hell happened to her?"

"She's getting her hair done," Mary laughed.

"What?" Rosie asked.

"Dale just appeared and he wondered about your outfit," Mary said.

"She looks like my TV antenna when we were trying to get better reception," Dale muttered.

"Mary, you didn't tell me there would be others at our meeting," Rosie complained.

"Rosie, I didn't know Dale would be here," Mary said apologetically. "But since he is here, he can help with the question at hand. Did they love him, er, you?"

"Nope, they didn't," he said, folding his arms over his chest. "They didn't love me at all."

"Dale doesn't think they loved him," Mary said to Rosie. "I disagree with him. I think they all loved him."

"So they didn't kill him?" Rosie asked.

"Well, I'm not willing to say that, yet," she said, "because sometimes you make bad decisions when you've got pressure from other areas. For example, did Jessie feel pressure from Quinn? Was there an 'If you love me you'll help me close this deal' moment? Was Josh feeling pressure about his future and saw this as a way to get out?"

"You still don't kill someone," Dale said. "No matter what you're feeling."

"Of course, I agree with you, Dale," Mary said. "But until I've found more information than I have right now, I can't give either you or Rosie a good answer."

Rosie sighed. "I really thought things would be figured out faster than this. On television it only takes those private eyes sixty minutes, with commercials."

Mary sighed and then thought of something. "I need to change the subject," she said, "Before you have to head back to the beauty shop. Do you remember hearing anything about a ghost in a yearbook when you were in high school?"

"You mean Dead Erika?" both Rosie and Dale said at the same time.

"Dead Erika?" Mary repeated. "Well, that's not very nice."

181

"Well, she was dead," Dale said.

"We only called her that because she was dead," Rosie said.

"How did she die?" Mary asked.

"Hit by a train," Dale replied.

"She committed suicide at the park," Rosie said.

"So, no one really knows," Mary said.

"All I know is that she died during her junior year of high school, before the pictures were taken and she showed up as a ghost," Rosie said.

"Yeah, yearbooks sales that year were off the books," Dale added. "They even got requests from folks out of town. Dead Erika put Freeport on the map that year."

Rosie looked down at her watch and then jumped up. "Oh, my time is almost up," she cried. "I need to get back, or I'll turn pink."

She turned, ran out the door and jogged down the sidewalk towards the beauty parlor.

"If that don't beat all," Dale said, slowing fading away. "I never did understand women."

Mary looked around her empty office, then stood up, walked over to the refrigerator and opened the freezer section. *Yep,* she thought, *this is going to be a two container kind of day.*

Chapter Twenty-eight

"Dead Erika," Bradley repeated, incredulously, trying not to smile as he watched Mary take her frustrations out on a pan of mashed potatoes. "They both actually called her Dead Erika?"

"People can be so insensitive when they are talking about dead people," Mary said, whipping butter into the softened potatoes. "I mean, what if she were in the room and heard them?"

Bradley came up behind her and slipped her arms around her waist. "Well, to be fair, most people don't expect dead people to be in the room listening," he said.

"Well, they should," she replied, beating the potatoes even harder. "I mean, even Dale said it, and he should know better."

"Well, it did happen while they were both kids," he said. "So, maybe they just said it without thinking. I'm sure Rosie would never intentionally say anything that would hurt someone's feelings."

The masher slowed in intensity and Mary sighed. "You're right," she said. "I don't know why I'm getting all worked up about it. It's like I can't control my emotions."

Then she leaned back against him and sighed. "And I have another confession to make," she said sadly, shaking her head when her emotions were too much for speech.

He turned her in his arms. "Mary?" he asked, concerned. "What's wrong?"

Big tears slipped down Mary's cheeks and she just shook her head. "I can't…"

Wiping away her tears, he kissed her tenderly. "You can tell me," he said. "No matter what…"

With a quivering lower lip, she finally was able to blurt out, "Three."

"Three?" Bradley asked. "Three? Is that right?"

She nodded, wiping away more tears with the back of her hand and grabbing a paper towel from the counter-top to blow her nose. "Three," she repeated.

"Three what, sweetheart?" he asked.

Her tears started up again. "Three containers," she sobbed, placing her head against his chest. He could barely hear her muffled, "Three whole containers."

"Of what?" he said, trying to be patient.

She dug her face further into his shoulder in mortification. "Ice cream," she muttered.

185

"What?" he asked, trying to lean in closer.

"Ice cream," she murmured again.

"What?"

She looked up at him. "Ice cream!" she shouted. "I ate three whole containers of ice cream today in my office."

"Three whole quarts?" he gasped.

She smacked his arm. "No, of course not," she said, offended. "I'm not a glutton. Three six-ounce containers."

"So, you're telling me that basically you ate three scoops of ice cream today and you're upset about it?" he asked.

She paused for a moment. "It seemed like more when they were in their own containers, she said slowly, feeling more than a little ridiculous.

He pulled her back into his arms and chuckled softly. "Were they good?"

She nodded. "That was the problem," she said. "They were delicious."

After kissing the top of her head, he laid his head on top of hers for a moment. "Really, three scoops is no big deal," he said soothingly. "And besides, dairy is good for you."

She relaxed against him and sighed. "Well, actually, it might have been four," she admitted. "I lost count after two."

Bradley pulled away and looked down at her, she was simply adorable. "Do we need an intervention?" he asked, trying not to smile.

"We might," she agreed, the side of her mouth lifting in a half-smile. "Is there a dark chocolate anonymous group I should sign up for?"

He paused for a moment and finally answered, "Oh, well, if it was dark chocolate, then it has antioxidants that are good for you and the baby."

She reached up and kissed him. "Have I told you lately how much I love you?" she asked.

"Well, you say that now," he agreed. "But tomorrow morning we start working out again."

"Working out?" she asked.

"Uh-huh, Krape Park at five-thirty," he said. "I understand exercise is vital for pregnant women."

"Five-thirty?" she gasped. "But how about my morning sickness?"

"I've read that exercise is great for morning sickness too," he added.

"You know what, Bradley Alden," she muttered.

He leaned forward and kissed the tip of her nose. "What Mary Alden?" he asked.

"You read way too much!"

Chapter Twenty-nine

"Can I have ice cream for dessert?" Clarissa asked as they sat around the table later that evening.

"Hmmm, well, I think we should ask your mother," Bradley said with a smirk. "She really is an expert on both ice cream and healthy eating habits."

She shot a quick glare at Bradley before turning to Clarissa with a smile. "Of course you can, sweetheart," she said. "What kind would you like?"

"Rocky Road," Clarissa called, "that's my favorite."

Bradley started to stand, but Mary delayed him, shaking her head. "No, please, let me get it," she said pointedly. "I need the exercise."

"Mary, I never said…"

She waved away his explanation. "No, really, that's okay," she said with a dramatic sigh. "I don't mind."

Chuckling, he reached over and helped himself to another spoonful of potatoes. "Well, as long as you don't mind," he teased.

"You are so insensitive," she said with a grin and got up and walked over to the refrigerator.

Mike leaned back against the kitchen wall. "I always loved ice cream," he said. "That's the one food I miss the most. Well, other than pizza, donuts and nachos."

"The four manly food groups," Bradley said.

Pulling the container of ice cream out of the freezer, Mary placed it on the counter and opened the lid. "How many scoops would you like?" she asked.

"Is two scoops too many?" Clarissa asked.

Mary shot Bradley a glare before he could even open his mouth. "Don't even," she warned.

He shrugged innocently and said, "What? I wasn't going to say a word."

"Two is fine," she said to Clarissa. "Two is perfect."

Clarissa looked back and forth between her parents and then glanced at Mike, who shrugged. "I don't know what's going on," he said.

She studied them for a little while longer and then finally said, "Remember, I'm going to see Dr. Springler tomorrow afternoon. Is there anything you want me to ask her for you?"

At first there was dead silence in the room. Mary froze in place, the ice cream scoop dripping onto the counter. Bradley turned in his chair and stared at his daughter. Finally Mike chuckled. Then

Mary and Bradley both started laughing at the same time.

Leaning against the counter, tears streaming down her face, Mary held her sides as the laughter hit her in waves. Dropping the scoop on the counter, she tried to pick up the bowl of ice cream, but just couldn't get her hands to work.

Bradley tried to stand, to help her, but couldn't gather the strength to stand up.

"Do they do this often?" Mike asked Clarissa.

Grinning, Clarissa shook her head. "Should I tell Dr. Springler?" she asked.

"She'd never believe you," he replied.

Looking at Mike, her guardian angel leaning against the kitchen wall and at her parents, weak with laughter, Clarissa decided there were a lot of things Dr. Springler would never believe.

Finally, after taking a deep breath for self-control, Mary was able to pick up the bowl of ice cream and carry it over to the table. "I'm so sorry, Clarissa," she wheezed. "For some reason, that was just so funny."

Sitting back against his chair, Bradley shook his head in agreement. "I think we're back to normal now."

Gliding over to sit in the empty chair, Mike shook his head. "You two were never normal," he said. "Don't pretend now."

Giggling and digging into her ice cream, Clarissa nodded. "That's okay though," she said. "Normal parents are boring."

"Well, we certainly aren't boring," Mary agreed and, seeing that Clarissa was relaxed and content, decided to inquire about her day. "So how was school today? Did you feel a little safer with the GPS device?"

With her mouth filled with Rocky Road, Clarissa nodded happily. "It was great," she mumbled around the ice cream. "I wasn't scared at all."

"That's great," Bradley said. "I'm so glad to hear it helped."

"Uh huh," she said, shoveling another spoonful into her mouth. "I only told Maggie about it, no one else. And I told her she could use it too, if any bad guys came."

"Well, that was a great idea," Mary said. "This way, both you and Maggie can feel safer."

"Yep," Clarissa agreed. "And we can use it when we have our business."

"Oh, what's your business going to be?" Bradley asked.

"Well, we're going to wait until we're a little bigger," she explained. "And then we're going to take over Mary's business, cause by then she'll be way too old and she'll have to raise the baby."

"Yeah, she's pretty old already," Mike said with a smirk.

"And what will you be doing with my business when I'm too old?" Mary asked.

"Maggie will see the ghosts and I'll help solve their mysteries," she said, and then she looked thoughtful for a moment. "You'll save us some, won't you?"

"Save you some?" Mary asked.

"Some ghosts," she said. "You won't solve all of their problems, will you?"

Mary laughed. "No, I think there will be plenty of ghosts left."

"As a matter of fact, your mother met a new ghost a couple of nights ago," Bradley said. "She was at Union Dairy and her name is Erika."

Mike turned to Mary, his eyes wide. "You met Dead Erika?"

"I can't believe you called her that," Mary replied.

"Well, her name is Erika and she's dead," he said. "That pretty much describes her."

"Wait, you know about Dead Erika?" Bradley asked, and then he quickly turned to Mary. "Sorry, his words, not mine."

"Yeah, my dad told me all about her," he said. "She showed up in her high school yearbook picture, like two months after she was dead."

"How did she die?" Mary asked.

Mike sat back in his chair. "Let me think," he said, looking up to the ceiling for a moment. "There are so many urban legends about her. She was drowned in the high school swimming pool, she fell off the catwalk at Jeannette-Lloyd Theater…"

"Could that have happened?" Bradley asked.

"Could have, if the theater had been built then," he replied.

"But what's the truth?" Mary asked. "How did she really die?"

"I don't know," Mike said. "And I don't know if anyone really does."

"How am I supposed to find out the truth?" Mary sighed.

"Why don't you just ask her," Clarissa said.

Mary paused and turned to Clarissa. "Well, why don't I?" she said, a smile growing on her face. "Clarissa, you and Maggie are going to be very successful when you take over my business."

Chapter Thirty

Mary slowly stood and walked over to the refrigerator, ignoring the freezer section, and pulled out a bottle of sparkling water. Placing the bottle on the top of the short office-sized appliance, she put both hands on the edge and stretched her legs behind her, groaning softly as her muscles tightened and then, finally, released. "I officially hate working out," Mary said.

"I'm sorry, what?" the man's voice behind her startled her into turning quickly and knocking her water bottle off the fridge and across the room, rolling to the feet of Quinn Edmonson.

"I'd pick it up for you," he said. "But as you can see, my arms are a little full."

Mary rushed forward; alarmed by the three file boxes he was balancing in his arms in the middle of her office. "Wait, don't move," she demanded. "It's right under your feet and I don't want you to stumble."

She grabbed the bottle and backed up quickly.

"Where would you like these?" he asked.

"These?" she responded.

"The files from the Maughold project," he replied. "I told you I'd let you borrow them."

She hurried over to her desk and pushed everything to one side, leaving a space large enough for the stacked boxes to sit. "Here, this is a great spot," she said.

Lowering the boxes to the desk, he slid them in place and stepped back, pulling a handkerchief out his slacks pocket and dabbing his forehead. "They were heavier than I thought," he said.

"Did you drive over?" Mary asked.

He shook his head. "No, my mistake," he said. "I thought it would be no big deal to carry them over. It's a very long two blocks from the bank to your office."

Mary nodded. "Very long," she agreed. "How about a bottle of water? I'll even get you one I haven't tossed across the room."

Smiling, he nodded as he sat in one of the chairs in front of Mary's desk. "That would be great," he said. "And, if you don't mind, I'd really like to hear any information you can share about the Johnson situation."

Mary grabbed another bottle of water and walked back to the desk. She handed him the bottle and then sat down across from him. Leaning back, she twisted the top off her bottle and took a drink and allowed him to do the same before she continued.

"You know, it's been an interesting case," she said, wondering how much she could really trust him. "I get the feeling that no one thinks Dale's death was an accident, but no one wants to betray anyone else."

"But wouldn't their father's murder be the ultimate betrayal?" he asked.

Mary met his eyes. "But when you love someone, you are often willing to commit that kind of betrayal," she said. "Even if it means the guilt makes you end the relationship."

He sat forward in his chair. "Are you saying Jessie thought I killed her father and ended the relationship because of it?"

Mary shrugged. "I think Jessie doesn't know who killed her dad," she said. "But I don't think she, or anyone else, believed he locked himself in that grain silo. So, I think she looked around at the people with motive and, although she never betrayed them, separated herself from them. She is no longer close to her brothers either."

Sighing, he shook his head. "Well, at least I'm in good company."

"So, tell me why I should believe you didn't kill Dale Johnson," Mary said. "Hypothetically, of course."

He actually smiled and nodded. "Of course."

"Well, on the one hand," Quinn began. "I really did want them to sell the land. It was my job to get this project done and, if I had done well, there was a promotion in it for me. And if I didn't get the sales..." He looked around and shrugged. "Well, I would be exactly where I am right now."

Mary studied him for a moment. He was a pleasant-looking man and, even though he was leaning toward middle-age paunch, she could tell he probably was on his high-school football team and had been very athletic. He was tall and broad shouldered, and carried himself more like a linebacker than a quarterback. She could see how Jessie would have been attracted to him. But did he use that attractiveness to manipulate her, or had he really cared for her?

"Okay, so you had motive," Mary finally said.

"Yeah, and I knew the farm pretty well," he added. "I was there when we had the surveyors there."

"Surveyors?" Mary asked.

"Yeah, every property had to have an official survey," he said. "So we could determine if we wanted to buy all of the land or just a section of it."

"So you went on all of the surveys?" she asked.

199

"Well, on all the properties I was responsible for," he said.

Mary shook her head and sat forward. "Wait, there was someone else buying properties for the project?"

"No," he said. "Well, I guess, yes, technically."

"Now I'm confused," she admitted.

He laughed. "I was the only person in the Freeport area buying properties, but I understand that some people were approached by corporate before I got here and made a deal with them. Kind of laying the ground work."

"Did you know which properties?" she asked.

"No, I didn't," he said. "There were so many properties in so many areas, I had no idea which direction the company was heading in. I just took each assignment and made appointments."

"So, do you know why they offered the Johnson's so much money for their property?" she asked.

He shook his head. "No, all I know is that they said something about it being a keystone property and it could make or break the deal."

"Okay, coming back to your guilt," Mary said. "This was make-or-break-the-deal property."

"Yeah, it was," he said. "And I talked to Dale Johnson until I was blue in the face. But, legacy was more important to him than money. There was nothing I could do to persuade him. When you check the files, you'll find a letter from me to corporate stating that the Johnson property was a no-go and they were going to have to re-evaluate things."

"When did you send that?" she asked.

"About a week before he died," Quinn replied. "But I still don't think they sent a hit man down from Chicago to take him out."

Mary nodded. "Yeah, neither do I," she admitted. "I will tell you that when I mentioned to Jessie that I spoke with you, she asked me how you were doing."

He sat up and grinned. "She did?"

"Yes, and she seemed a little distracted for a while," Mary added. "Not like someone who was no longer interested, if you know what I mean."

"Why are you telling me this?" he asked. "I could be the bad guy."

"My gut tells me you're not the bad guy," she said. "And if I'm going to solve this one, I have a feeling I'm going to need some help."

He stood and leaned over her desk, offering her his hand. "You've got it," he said. "Whatever I can do, just let me know. And when it's over…"

"Yes?"

He smiled shyly. "If I have my way, I'll invite you to the wedding."

She stood up, took his hand and shook it. "I'll be there," she said. "With bells on."

Chapter Thirty-one

Mary looked up from the tenth folder and slowly rolled her head, getting all the kinks out of her neck. She reached over, without looking, and lifted her bottle of water to her lips, only to find it dry. "Dang, when did that happen?" she murmured.

She turned to her computer screen, looked at the time and sat up straight in her chair. "Crap!" she cried, grabbing her phone and dialing Rosie's number.

Rosie answered on the first ring. "Rosie Wagner."

"Rosie, this is Mary and I am so sorry," she said. "I got caught up in the case and didn't watch the time. I know I was supposed to meet you for lunch."

Mary could hear Rosie's laughter through the phone. "So you really didn't see me, did you?" she asked.

"See you?"

"I stood outside your office building and waved my hand like a looney-bird," she explained. "When you still didn't budge, I figured you were caught up, so I got us lunch to go. How do roast beef sandwiches on hard rolls sound?"

"Amazing," Mary said, realizing she really was hungry. "Um, did they include pickles?"

"Of course," Rosie laughed. "Big deli dill pickles and some of the cheese and pea salad you like."

"Oh, Rosie, you are the best friend anyone could ever have," she said. "When will you be here?"

"I'm coming up the sidewalk now," she said. "I'll be there in a moment."

True to her word, a moment later Rosie entered Mary's office with a shopping bag filled with their lunch. "What's that?" she asked, pointing to the stack of boxes.

"Quinn brought those over," Mary said, shifting them over so there was a place for the food. "They're the files for the Maughold project."

"Well, that was very nice of him," Rosie said, picking up a file and glancing through it. "This is really good information."

Mary nodded as she pulled the food out of the bag. "He's been very helpful," Mary said. "And he's willing to help in whatever way he can to help figure this out. He still has feelings for Jessie."

Rosie closed the file and met Mary's eyes. "Does he realize that if he helps us figure out that one of Jessie's brothers is the killer, she might not return his feelings?"

Mary paused and took a deep breath. "You know, I don't think that occurred to either of us," she admitted. "I hope I don't end up ruining his chances with Jessie."

"Well, the most important thing is the truth," Rosie said. "Isn't it?"

"I think so, you think so, but I don't know if the Johnson family thinks so," she said. "They've been pretty good at avoiding the truth for fifteen years."

They both sat down on either side of the desk and unwrapped their sandwiches. Mary took a large bite of hers and closed her eyes in pleasure. "Oh, Rosie, this is just what I needed," she said.

"You do need to remember to eat," Rosie admonished. "Not only does your body need it, but if you go too long without food, you'll get morning sickness."

"In the afternoon?" Mary asked. "Isn't it officially afternoon sickness then?"

"Most women will tell you that morning sickness is actually morning-noon-and night sickness," Rosie replied, lifting up a carrot stick and pointing it at Mary for emphasis. "And you don't want to go there."

"So, now that you're here, eating with me," Mary said. "How would you like to review some of these files with me?"

"Sure, my afternoon is free," she said. "And the sooner we figure out what happened to Dale, the sooner I can sell that house."

"Excellent," Mary said, passing Rosie a ten-inch stack of files. "You can start on these."

"What am I looking for?" she asked.

"Well, so far the Johnson farm is the only one that seems to have been given the incentive offer that multiplied the value of their land," Mary said. "I want to see if there are any other parcels with a similar offer."

"Okay, anything else?" she asked.

"No. I really can't think of anything else to look for," she said. "But if you stumble on anything unusual, let me know."

Rosie pulled out her phone. "When do we need to stop?" she asked. "I'll set an alarm, so you're not late for something else."

Mary laughed. "Actually, Bradley is picking Clarissa up for her appointment with Dr. Springler this afternoon and then they're going grocery shopping together," she said. "So I'm free until about five. It will probably be pizza night at the Alden household; do you and Stanley want to come by?"

"That would be fun," she said. "I'll let Stanley know."

Mary pulled her keyboard towards her. "And I'll let Bradley know, before I forget," she said.

Several hours later, the remnants of lunch still on the desk, Mary placed the last file back in the box and shook her head. "I don't see anything in these files that would suggest anything unusual, to say nothing about corrupt," she said. "Quinn took very careful notes and documented everything."

"And the letter he sent to corporate about the Johnson property is factual and professional," Rosie added. "There's nothing to suggest that he was going to try and persuade Dale to do anything he didn't want to do."

Mary chewed her lower lip. "Okay, so what's the next step?" she asked. "We still don't have a valid reason why the Johnson farm was so important."

"This is like a big jigsaw puzzle," Rosie said.

Looking up quickly, Mary smiled at her friend. "Rosie, that's brilliant," she said.

"What?" Rosie asked, confused.

"A jigsaw puzzle," Mary said. "Quinn told me that every parcel had a survey done. So, let's put all

207

the pieces together to see why the Johnson property is so important."

"Oh, that's a great idea," she said. "I have a couple of large folding tables. I'll bring them tonight and then we can all work on it."

"Great, pizza and a puzzle," Mary said. "Sounds like a fun night."

"Let's put these back in the boxes and I'll help you carry them to your car," Rosie suggested. "And then, hopefully, tonight we will solve the case."

Chapter Thirty-two

"There's one more piece of pepperoni," Bradley called from the kitchen. "Any takers?"

"Well, iffen no one else is gonna bite, I will," Stanley said, grabbing his paper plate and carrying into the kitchen. "I got room for one more piece."

Walking past Clarissa who was at the kitchen table coloring, he paused and patted her head. "Whatcha drawing there, sweetheart?" he asked.

"A ghost my mom saw at Union Dairy," she explained. "I can't draw ghost pictures at school because my mom and dad think people might not understand. Even Dr. Springler thinks I probably shouldn't talk about them at school too."

Bradley's head shot up and he met Mary's face, wide-eyed and concerned. "Did you have a nice visit with Dr. Springler today?" Bradley asked.

Clarissa nodded. "Yes, she was nicer to me today," she said. "Especially after I told her about what Maggie and I want to do when we grow up. But she was a little confused."

"In what way?" Bradley asked, watching Mary get up from the couch and walk towards the kitchen.

Sighing, Clarissa put down one crayon and picked up another. "She didn't understand about ghosts at all. She didn't think Mom and Maggie could do that," she said. "She thought I was saying something bad about Mom."

"What did she say?" Mary asked.

"She said that I needed to not make things up about you," Clarissa said. "And that I should love you for who you are and not for a make believe job I pretend you have."

Coming forward and slipping her arms around Clarissa, Mary held her tightly. "I'm so sorry she didn't believe you," Mary said. "I should have thought about that."

"Did I do bad?" Clarissa asked. "You said I should tell her everything I was thinking about. That I should be honest with her."

"Yes we did," Mary said. "And you did nothing wrong at all."

She looked up at Bradley. "And tomorrow I'll go in and explain everything to her," she said.

Clarissa wrapped her arms around Mary. "Good, 'cause she was saying she might need to talk to the school counselor about my pretending," Clarissa said. "And then that would spoil our secret."

Mary nodded. "Yes, it would spoil our secret," she said. "I'll call her first thing in the morning and get in to see her, I promise."

"Maybe you could also ask Gracie to give her a call," Bradley suggested. "One shrink to another."

"Yes, that's a good idea," Mary replied and she bent and kissed Clarissa on the top of her head. "Sorry sweetheart."

Clarissa shrugged. "There's no reason to be sorry," Clarissa said. "I get to have my own guardian angel and you help people become angels. That's the coolest job any mom could ever have."

Smiling, Mary gave her another hug. "I totally agree."

"So, what's the name of this ghost you're drawing?" Stanley asked, biting into the pizza.

"Dead Erika," Clarissa said.

Bradley stifled his chuckle and Mary rolled her eyes. "Clarissa…," she began.

"Erika Arnold," Stanley interrupted, looking at Mary. "You're helping Erika Arnold?"

"You know her?" Mary asked.

"Yeah, we went to school together," he replied. "She still hasn't moved on?"

"No, she's at Union Dairy, waiting for a ride," she said. "I think she said she was waiting for Adam."

Stanley placed the pizza down on his plate and shook his head. "Well, she ain't gonna get the ride she wants," he said. "Adam died in the same crash she died in."

"How come she doesn't know that?" Clarissa asked.

Mary looked at her daughter. "That's a very good question."

"From what I remember, they were both in the car when it crashed," Stanley said. "They were driving out on Highway 75, northeast of town. The weather was bad, the roads were slick and Adam was driving too dang fast. The sheriff's deputy seemed to think they both died immediately."

"Do you remember where the crash was?" Mary asked.

Stanley nodded. "Yeah, right past the curve near Winneshiek Road."

"Thanks," Mary said. "I'll check it out."

Looking from Stanley to Mary, Clarissa asked, "Do you like helping ghosts?"

"Yes, I do," she replied. "I like it very much."

Yawning, she smiled at her mother. "I think Maggie and I are going to like it too," she said.

"And I think you will both be very good at it," Mary said, giving Clarissa another quick hug. "Now let's get you upstairs and ready for bed. You look exhausted."

Slipping out of the chair, Clarissa rubbed her eyes. "I am pretty tired," she agreed.

She went around the room, giving all of the adults hugs, and then took Mary's hand to walk upstairs.

"I'll be up in a bit to read to you," Bradley promised.

"Okay," she replied, yawning again.

"I don't think you'll get much reading done tonight," Rosie said with a smile.

"Darn," Bradley grinned. "And we were just getting to the good part."

In two quick bites, Stanley finished his piece of pizza and walked over to the sink to wash his hands. After drying them on the towel, he turned to Rosie and Bradley. "Why don't we get started on those surveys?" he asked. "Seems to me Mary is going to have a busy day tomorrow."

Bradley and Stanley unfolded the large folding tables and set them up in the middle of the living room. The combination of the two gave them a working space of five feet by six feet.

Rosie went through the box and pulled out the Johnson file. "Let's put this survey in the center and build around it," she suggested.

"Okay, great idea," Bradley said. "Which one is next?"

By the time Mary came down the stairs, the tables were full of surveys taped on the corners with masking tape. "Wow, good job," she said. "Is this all of them?"

"These are the ones adjacent to the Johnson property," Bradley said. "Now don't solve the case until I come back down." Giving Mary a quick kiss on the cheek, he hurried upstairs to read to Clarissa.

Mary smiled and shook her head, then turned back to the table. "So, we have these all laid out," she said. "Does it make sense that the Johnson farm was considered a keystone spot?"

"Well, iffen this piece were here, it would make more sense," Stanley said, pointing to a large bare spot on the table next to the Johnson survey.

"That must be Sawyer Gartner's place," Mary said. "He was on the county board at the time. He wasn't selling his property."

"How do you know?" Stanley asked. "I've known Sawyer for a long time and I can't see him passing up an opportunity to make some money."

"He would have to have recused himself from the county board proceedings," Mary said. "And from what I understand, he was on the committee who decided whether or not the project went through."

"It's strange," Rosie said, flipping through a multi-page document. "This lists all the properties in the project, but we're missing one."

"Does it give a name we should be looking for?" Mary asked, moving closer and reading over Rosie's shoulder.

"No, the only one I can't figure out is this trust," Rosie said. "All of the others are listed by owner name."

"Well, Quinn did say there were some properties their corporate offices were handling," she said.

"We got a puzzle with a missing piece," Stanley said. "Could be property that somehow connects to the Johnson place, and that would give us a better idea."

"I'll call Quinn in the morning and see if he can get that file," Mary said.

"You might want to check the county board meeting records," Stanley suggested. "Maybe something was mentioned there about the Johnson place. It would have been under the Rural Development subcommittee and at the time would have been a closed meeting because of the sensitivity of the payments to each landowner. But after ten years, the Freedom of Information Act kicks in, so there shouldn't be a problem."

"I'll see if I can find any sales records referencing this trust number," Rosie suggested. "We might have something in the old MLS files."

Bradley came down the stairs as Rosie and Stanley were slipping on their coats. "Did you solve it when I was upstairs?" he asked with an exaggerated sigh.

Rosie walked over and patted him on his cheek. "No, darling," she said. "We just have more questions."

"Questions?" he asked, looking at Mary.

She smiled. "Don't worry, dear, I'll tell you all about it."

Chapter Thirty-three

Mary got in early to the office the next day. After a refreshing early morning jog— that she hated to admit she actually enjoyed— she showered, dressed and grabbed some food before she hurried off to the office. Bradley planned on getting into the office late that morning, so he helped Clarissa get on her way.

"Don't forget to call Dr. Springler," Clarissa reminded her after she kissed her daughter goodbye.

"I won't," Mary promised. "I'll call her as soon as I get in."

After setting up her laptop, she pulled out her phone and made the call she was actually dreading. *Really*, she thought as she listened to the ringing at the other end of the line, *I am getting tired of being labelled a nut case. So what if I see ghosts? So what if I have a guardian angel with a wicked sense of humor living in my house? Can't we all just accept people for who we are?*

"Dr. Springler's office," the voice on the other end of the line said. "May I help you?"

"Yes, hi, this is Mary O'Reilly, um, I mean Mary Alden," she said.

Great, now they're going to think I have a multiple personality disorder, she thought.

"I was hoping to meet with Dr. Springler for a few minutes today," she continued aloud.

"Oh, Mrs. Alden," the voice on the other end of the line replied. "Yes, I know she wanted to speak with you."

Okay, yep, they've talked about me.

"When would she like to meet?" Mary asked.

"Well, she is booked solid all day," her receptionist replied. "But she felt it was important enough to skip lunch, if you want to come by then."

Oh, not only am I a nut, I'm making her starve too.

"Why don't you suggest she meet me for lunch," Mary said. "My treat. How about Union Dairy?"

"Well, that's highly irregular," she replied.

Well, I'm highly irregular, Mary thought.

"It would be very helpful and because of my pregnancy, I really shouldn't be skipping any meals," Mary said, pleased with herself that she thought of the pregnancy angle.

"Hold on a moment, let me ask her."

Mary tapped the end of her pencil against her desk top as she wondered what she was going to say to the good doctor. *Really, it's nothing, I see dead people. A funny thing happened to me on the way to heaven. No, really, I'm on a mission from God.* She shook her head. "No, this is not going to be easy."

"I beg your pardon?" the receptionist asked.

"Oh, nothing," Mary stammered. "I have a client in my office." And she purposefully lowered her voice. "I'll be with you in a moment."

Then she said brightly, "Sorry, what did the doctor say?"

"The doctor will be happy to meet you at Union Dairy at noon," she replied.

"Thank you," Mary said. "I'll see her then. Goodbye."

After hanging up, she sat back in her chair and exhaled loudly.

"What's the problem?" Dale asked, appearing before her desk.

"Oh, nothing," Mary said. "Just a child psychologist who thinks I'm a couple buns short of a dozen because I can see ghosts."

Dale chuckled. "You want me to go over and haunt her office?" he asked and then he paused. "Can I do that? Haunt things?"

219

Mary grinned and nodded. "Yes, you can," she said. "At least that's what I've been told. You just have to concentrate on making yourself be seen and then you can appear."

"Maybe I'll pay a visit to some of my kids," he mused. "Scare the crap out of them."

"Well, before you do that, we ought to be sure they deserve having the crap scared out of them."

"What have you learned so far?" he asked.

"That none of the other properties I have the files on were given anything close to what you were given for your land," she said. "And the location of the properties don't seem to do anything to make your property that important."

"Did they pay for any of the other sites?" he asked.

"No," she said, shaking her head. "As a matter of fact, none of them even had a contract written up with a contingency on the board's approval."

"Don't you think that's strange?" he asked. "Wouldn't you think that once the board approved the project, those properties would be worth more?"

Mary nodded. "Yes, and if you were looking to purchase all of those plots, wouldn't you want

220

something signed by both parties agreeing to the terms?"

"Looks like a smokescreen to me," he said.

"Smokescreen?"

"Yeah, you do a bunch of stuff over here to keep folks eyes off of what you're doing right in front of their faces," he said.

"Now all we've got to do is figure that out," she said.

"Yeah, but don't worry," he said with a smile, as he began to fade away. "I've got confidence in you."

Chapter Thirty-four

"Hi Quinn, it's Mary O'Reilly," she said. "I went through the files yesterday and I have some questions for you."

"Sure, Mary, what do you need?" Quinn asked.

"Well, first, if there is any way to get our hands on that last folder, the one corporate handled, it would be very helpful," she said. "There seems to be still quite a few questions about why the Johnson property was so important."

"Okay, let me make a couple calls and see what I can get," he said. "What else?"

"Well, this might be obvious to you," she said. "But why aren't there any signed contracts in the folders?"

"Because we didn't make any offers until we knew the project was approved," he said.

"But wouldn't the owners decide their property was worth more once the project was approved?" she asked.

Quinn was silent on the other end of the phone for a few moments. "You know, this was my first job," he said. "And I really just followed what my manager in Chicago told me to do. But, now that you mention it, it doesn't make sense that we didn't have all those folks signed under a contingency contract."

"Okay, we're both on the same page here then. Do you think they talked to all these other owners as a kind of a smokescreen?" she asked, using Dale's term.

She was met with another moment of silence. "So, you're suggesting they had me talk to all of these other property owners to get some excitement growing about the project so there was community support?" he finally asked.

"I don't know," she said. "I'm just wondering why they bought the Johnson property upfront and no one else even had a contract."

"Yeah, you've got me wondering too," Quinn said. "Let me see what I can find out. Are you going to be in your office this afternoon?"

"Yes, I've got some errands this morning and a lunch meeting," she replied. "But I'll be back here after that."

"Okay, I'll be by this afternoon," he said. "And Mary…"

"Yes, Quinn."

"You've really got me wondering about this whole project."

Mary sat back in her office chair and nodded. "Yeah, you're not the only one."

A few minutes later, Mary was entering the Stephenson County Clerk's office. She walked to the counter and immediately saw her good friend, Linda.

With a delighted smile, Linda came from behind her glass-walled office and met Mary at the counter. "Hi, how's married life?" she asked.

"Oh, it's amazing," Mary said. "As you well know."

Linda nodded. "Oh, yes, I know, thanks to you," she said. "We're going to have to invite you, Bradley and Clarissa over for dinner soon."

"That would be great," Mary said.

"So, what can I do for you?" Linda asked.

"I'm looking for some minutes from the County Board Rural Development subcommittee meetings," Mary said. "They're from about fifteen years ago, though."

"Fifteen years ago," Linda said. "We've scanned a lot of those documents and they are now on the server. Do you know some keywords I can use to search for your documents?"

"Sure, how about starting with Maughold," Mary suggested.

"Oh, yeah, the Maughold project," Linda said, nodding her head. "That's enough of a keyword. What do you want?"

"Any of the meetings of the subcommittee," Mary said. "Is that too much?"

"Nope, no problem," Linda said. "It'll take me a little while to open up all the folders and print everything out. I can drop it off at your office after lunch."

"No, I don't want you to go through any trouble for me," Mary said.

"No trouble," Linda assured her. "I have to go past your office after lunch anyway. Okay?"

"Actually, that would be great," Mary agreed. "I have a lunch meeting, but I should be back soon after one. Does that work?"

"If you're not there, I'll just slide the envelope through your mail slot."

"Perfect, thanks Linda," she said.

"No problem," Linda said. "And I'll call you next week about dinner."

Chapter Thirty-five

Mary decided to walk to Union Dairy rather than drive the four blocks, the sun was out and the weather was warm. As she got closer, she saw Dr. Springler get out of her car in front of the ice cream parlor. *Great! I'm going to be late*; she groaned silently and hurried forward. She was just about to call to the doctor, when she noticed the woman's face and stopped in her tracks. The woman looked frightened, as if she was afraid to go inside. *Did the doctor have phobias of her own?* Mary wondered.

Walking closer, she kept studying the woman as she hesitated; seemingly arguing with herself about entering. Mary paused a few feet away and waited for the doctor to make up her mind. The woman stepped up and grasped the steel push bar on the door, but then stepped back quickly and shook her head. Mary tried to step back, out of her line of sight, but she moved too slowly and the doctor's eyes widened when she saw Mary.

"Hello," Mary said with false brightness. "Thanks so much for meeting me here."

The doctor took a deep breath and pasted a smile on her face. "Oh, you're welcome," she said quickly. "I, um, I haven't been here in quite a while."

"Well, it hasn't changed," Mary said with a smile, pulling the door open. "After you."

After a quick inhaled breath, Dr. Springler smiled at Mary and the preceded her into the restaurant.

"Shall we take a booth in the back?" Mary asked. "That will give us a little more privacy."

"That would be fine," she replied. "There is something I need to speak with you about that does require a modicum of confidentiality."

"Yes, I heard about that," Mary said, leading the way into the back room. "Here, why don't we take this corner booth?"

The back room was fairly empty; the only other customers were a group of four women sitting several seats away. Dr. Springler looked around the room and then nodded. "Yes, this will be fine."

Soon after taking a seat, a young waitress approached them and took their order. With a promise their food would be delivered soon, she left the women to visit in privacy.

"Mrs. Alden," Dr. Springler said, leaning forward in the booth and lowering her voice. "Clarissa shared some fairly disturbing information with me yesterday that I felt needed to be discussed immediately. I'm grateful you called this morning."

227

Mary nodded. "When Clarissa told us what she had discussed with you, I thought it would be wise to set up this meeting as soon as possible."

"You do understand that lying to your daughter is not a wise thing to do," Dr. Springler said. "No matter how harmless you may think a little fantasy is, it is still a lie."

"Dr. Springler, I don't lie to my daughter," Mary replied. "We are very honest with her."

Dr. Springler shook her head. "Are you telling me that you believe you can communicate with dead people, Mrs. Alden?"

"Hi Mary!"

Mary turned quickly to see Brandon standing next to her booth and then turned back to the doctor.

"Mrs. Alden?" the doctor prompted.

"I'm sorry," Mary said. "I was distracted for a moment. But, to tell you the truth…"

"You found her!" Brandon cried, his eyes filling with tears. "You found my mom, just like you said you would."

Mary turned again and found Brandon staring at Dr. Springler.

"Mrs. Alden, is there something wrong?" the doctor demanded.

"Dr. Springler, I'm so sorry, but I have to ask you," Mary said. "Did you have a son?"

Dr. Springler sat straight up in her seat and shook her head. "I don't see how that has anything to do with the subject we were discussing," she said.

"Actually, I think it has a great deal to do with it," Mary countered. "Brandon has been waiting for you to come back here. He's been looking for you."

Dr. Springler's face turned white and her lips thinned. "I don't know what kind of charlatan you are, Mrs. Alden," she spat. "But using a dead child to influence a mother is not only cruel and abusive, it's sick. The kind of sick that should not be influencing a child."

She started to stand, but Mary placed her hand on her arm and held her in the booth. "Just give me a moment to explain," Mary insisted. "A moment can't hurt anything."

"Why is my mom so angry?" Brandon asked, his voice shaking.

"She thinks I'm lying to her," Mary said. "She thinks I'm telling her you're here to make her sad."

"Tell her to remember what she always said to me," Brandon said.

"Brandon just asked me to tell you to remember what you always said to him," Mary said.

"What I always said to him," she repeated.

"When people die you just have to go back to the places you went to with them and you'll find them there," Brandon said. "I came back here, but you never did."

"He said that you told him when people die, you just have to go back to the places you went with them and you'll find them there," she repeated. "That's why his spirit came here. He wanted to see you again."

Dr. Springler's eyes filled with tears and she shook her head. "How could you know that?" she asked. "Who told you about my son?"

"Brandon told me," Mary said. "He told me that he and his mom would come here after they went to the library. He also told me that you both spent a lot of time at the hospital."

Dr. Springler looked away and wiped her eyes. "He was very sick," she said, her voice trembling. "He died of cancer."

"I'm so sorry," Mary said softly.

"Tell her I'm okay," he said.

"He said to tell you he's okay," Mary said.

"But I miss her," Brandon added. "Everyday. That's why I came here, to find her."

Mary's voice shook a little and she swallowed before she tried to speak. "He said he missed you, so he came here, to find you."

"This can't be real," Dr. Springler insisted. "This is a game."

"It's not a game," Mary said, meeting Dr. Springler's eyes. "It's a responsibility that I take very seriously. I don't lie, I don't fabricate and I don't take advantage of anyone. But I do have the ability to see the spirits of those who have passed away."

"I don't believe you."

"Well, then, test me," Mary said. "Ask me a question that only Brandon would know. That no amount of research or trickery could find."

"I don't want to play games with you."

"So, you would rather brand me an unfit mother and a liar than face your own fears?" Mary asked. "Somehow that doesn't seem fair either."

"Fine," she snapped. "Ask Brandon the name of his favorite pet."

Mary turned to Brandon. "Brandon, what's the name of your favorite pet?"

Giggling, Brandon shook his head. "She's trying to trick you," he said. "I couldn't have pets 'cause I was too sick. So, I had my dinosaurs. My favorite dinosaur was Tex, the T-Rex."

Mary turned to Dr. Springler. "Brandon said he couldn't have pets, because he was too sick," Mary said. "So, instead, you got him dinosaurs and his favorite was Tex, the T-Rex."

She shook her head as tears streamed down her face. "It can't be," she whispered. "It can't be."

Mary pulled a twenty out of her purse and left it on the table. "Why don't the three of us go right outside to the park?" Mary suggested. "It's even more private out there, and then you and Brandon can have a better conversation."

Grabbing a napkin to blot her eyes, she nodded and followed Mary out the door. They walked to a small bench next to the Lincoln-Douglas Debate site and sat down. Dr. Springler turned to Mary. "How do you?"

"That's not important right now," Mary said. "But I will explain it to you later. Now, you and Brandon need to talk. I don't know how long he has to visit with you."

"Brandon?" she asked. "Is it really you?"

"Yeah, Mom," he said. "I'm glad you finally showed up."

232

Mary relayed Brandon's answer to his mom and she shook her head. "I don't understand," she said. "He's dead. He's gone. I never thought…"

"Mom, you were too sad," Brandon said. "You closed off your heart. Grandma and I were worried about you, so I came back."

Surprised by Brandon's statement, Mary just sat for a moment. "You don't need help moving on?" she finally asked the little boy. "You've already been to the light?"

Brandon nodded. "It's my fault she's sad," he said. "So I had to come back."

Turning to Dr. Springler, Mary shook her head. "I don't think this has happened to me before," she said. "Usually the spirits I help are stuck here because of some unfinished business. But your son came back. He'd already moved on, but he came back because he thinks it's his fault you closed off your heart."

"I didn't…," Dr. Springler began and then she paused, covering her mouth with her hand. Nodding slowly, she took a deep breath. "I did," she whispered, surprised by her own words. "I did close my heart off. It hurt so badly to lose him. He was my baby. I loved him so much. And then, he was gone."

"So, if you closed off your heart, did you think you would never be hurt again?" Mary asked.

233

"I don't know if I even thought it that far through," she confessed. "I just hurt, so I retreated. But I never allowed myself to open up again."

"Mom, I'm not gone," Brandon insisted. "You just can't see me for now. But, just like you said, I'm always at the places we used to go. You need to go there and remember."

"Brandon says that's he not gone, it's just that you can't see him. But if you go to the places you both used to share, you'll remember him," Mary said.

"It hurts to remember," she said.

"Then you're remembering the wrong stuff," Brandon insisted.

Mary smiled slightly. "Brandon says then you're remembering the wrong stuff," Mary repeated.

"Can he keep coming to you?" she asked. "Can he be there when I come? Can it be like he hasn't died?"

Brandon looked at Mary as he listened to his mother's plea and his face dropped. "No, Mom," Brandon said. "I only got this one time to talk to you like this. You have to keep living, I already moved to where I'm supposed to be. But you still have stuff you need to do."

Mary took a deep breath and replied to Dr. Springler. "No, Brandon only has this one time to talk to you. He says that he's where he's supposed to be and you need to keep living. It's not your time to be together with him. There are still things you need to do."

"Only one time?" she asked. "That doesn't seem fair, does it? God takes away my son and I only get one time to talk with him and tell him how I feel?"

"No, Mom, you get forever," he said. "But you have to wait a little while for that. Just for now you have to remember the good stuff and how much I love you. Then you just have to do all you can until it's your turn to come and live with me."

"You don't only get one time, you get forever," Mary repeated. "Brandon will be waiting to greet you on the other side, when it's your turn. But until then, he's asking you to remember the good times and how much he loves you."

"He still loves me?" she asked. "Even though he's dead?"

"Mom," Brandon replied, rolling his eyes at her question. "Love is much stronger than death."

"Brandon said that love is stronger than death," Mary said, nodding her head. "And he's right, believe me, I know."

A few minutes later, as she watched Dr. Springler's car pull away from the curb, Mary prayed that the woman would be able to reconcile everything she'd experienced and feel some joy in her life.

"She'll be okay, right?" Brandon asked, as he stood beside her on the grass.

"Well, it's up to her," Mary said. "But I think you made a difference. She needed to hear from you."

"Will you do me another favor?" he asked.

"Sure, what do you want?"

"Pick some dandelions for her," he said. "They were her most favorite flower."

Mary smiled at Brandon and nodded. "I'll be sure to do that," she promised. "And I'll tell her they're from you."

"Thanks Mary," he said, as he slowly faded away. "Thanks a lot."

Chapter Thirty-six

Mary held the take-out bag from Union Dairy in her hand and hurried down the street. What was she thinking not driving her car? She was incredibly grateful to the waitress who saw them go outside and put their orders in to-go bags. Mary brought the bag up to her nose and sniffed. That young woman deserved a medal.

She turned the corner onto Main Street and rolled her eyes. Just as she had suspected, there was a line outside her door. Linda, Quinn, Rosie and Stanley were all waiting for her.

She hurried forward, her key in hand and smiled. "Hi, sorry I'm late," she said.

"You didn't even get time to eat?" Stanley asked.

"No, we kind of got involved," Mary replied, opening the door and holding it for everyone. "So, I took mine with me."

"Well, sit down and eat," Stanley growled. "A woman in your condition needs to eat."

"Mary, are you…?" Linda asked with a smile.

"Yeah, she's pregnant, but no one's supposed to know," Stanley interrupted.

Mary chuckled. "Yes, Linda, I'm pregnant," she said. "But it's early still, so we were keeping it quiet for a little while longer."

"Yeah, like I said, no one's supposed to know," Stanley said. "So, who told you anyway?"

Rolling her eyes, Rosie patted Stanley's arm. "Don't worry, dear, I'll tell you later."

Leaning forward, Linda gave Mary a hug. "Well, congratulations," she said. "And don't worry, I won't tell a soul. In the meantime, here are the minutes you needed."

"Thank you," Mary said, taking the envelope and placing it on her desk. "You really didn't need to wait."

"Well, I wanted you to know that someone else also requested copies of those minutes," she said.

"Who?" Mary asked.

"Josh Johnson," she replied. "It was so strange that out of the blue he would ask for copies too, that I thought you might want to know."

"Thank you," Mary said. "That is very interesting."

"Okay, I've got to run," Linda said. "Good luck with the rest of your afternoon."

Once Linda left, Stanley leaned against the wall and folded his arms. "Well, I guess that's that," he said. "Josh must've killed his dad."

"Well, before you jump to any conclusions, you might want to see this," Quinn said, holding out an envelope for Mary.

She pulled out the contents and scanned them. "But this can't be right," she said.

"Yeah, that's what I thought," Quinn said.

"You mean you found out that Sawyer Gartner's property was the missing link?" Rosie asked, holding out a manila folder.

"Is this the paperwork for the sale to Maughold?" Mary asked.

Rosie shook her head. "No, actually, this is the paperwork from the purchase of his property from Maughold after the project fell through."

Mary sat down at her desk. "What?"

"He bought back his property two months after the project was cancelled," Rosie said. "He used a different trust account, so it would have been hard to trace."

Mary flipped through the paperwork Quinn had just handed her and found the sale contract. "Okay, here's the addendum," she said. "In the case the project wasn't realized, he had the right to buy back his property at current land values."

"Did he sell the property at current land values?" Rosie asked.

"No, he sold each acre for $25,000," Mary said.

"That's more like residential acreage, not farm land," Rosie said. "And he only paid $2,500 to buy it back."

"Why would anyone agree to those kind of terms?" Mary wondered aloud.

"Well, iffen you thought you had a done deal," Stanley said. "Or you were partnering with someone to make some extra money."

Chapter Thirty-seven

There was complete silence in the room for a few moments; everyone just stared at each other, contemplating the enormity of Stanley's words. Suddenly, the office door burst open and Josh Johnson strode inside shaking an envelope in Mary's face.

"This will prove Abe had nothing to do with my father's death," he shouted.

"Well, this certainly is a day for envelopes, isn't it," Rosie said calmly. "I'm so glad I thought to be unique and bring my damning information in a manila folder."

Josh froze and looked around the room at the rest of the group gathered there. "I, um, I apologize," he stammered, until he saw Quinn standing in the corner of the room. "You! I might have known that you would be involved in a plot to hurt my family again."

Mary took a quick longing look at her already cold lunch and sighed. Then she noticed that Dale Johnson had appeared in the middle of the room and seemed to be enjoying the ruckus. Sending a disapproving glance in Dale's direction, she finally stood up. "Actually, Josh, Quinn has been helping me get to the bottom of your father's murder," she said, raising her voice above the din. "At your father's request."

Once again, a fragile silence fell upon the office.

"Come again?" Josh asked.

"Your father is my client," Mary said. "He asked me to get to the bottom of his murder."

"What are you, a psychic sleuth?" he scoffed.

"Well, Mary, that has a nice ring to it," Rosie commented. "You might consider changing your title."

"Naw, it would be too hard for people with lisps," Stanley replied.

"What the hell?" Josh cried. "Are you people never serious?"

"We're serious," Mary replied. "Dead serious." But then, she couldn't help herself, she giggled. "I'm sorry, that sounded so lame."

Josh threw the envelope on the floor and was going to storm out when Dale said, "He never did have a sense of humor."

"Your dad says you never did have a sense of humor," Mary called, stopping Josh cold.

"I remember the time I played an April Fool's joke on him," Dale continued. "Rushed into his bedroom with a broom and told him to stay in his bed. I'd take care of the raccoon."

"Remember the April Fool's joke with the raccoon?" Mary asked.

Josh turned around and stared, opened mouthed, at her.

"He nearly peed the bed," Dale said, chuckling. "Didn't think it was funny at all when I called out April Fool's."

"Your dad remembers you not thinking it was very funny," she added.

"It wasn't funny," he replied. "Not as funny as the time we replaced his sugar bowl with salt."

Gliding over to his son, Dale started to laugh. "It was a good joke," he admitted. "And I was a spoil sport. Made those poor boys muck out the dairy barn for two weeks."

"Your dad said he was a spoil sport and he made you and Abe muck out the dairy barn for two weeks," Mary said with a smile. "He did admit it was a good joke."

Josh grinned. "The screwed up look on his face when he gulped down coffee with three salts was worth the time in the barn," he laughed. "Abe and I laughed about his face for months."

Then he froze and looked at Mary. "How did you know that?" he asked.

Mary shrugged. "Your dad is here," she said. "In my office. He just told me."

Quinn looked around the room with panic in his eyes and Rosie took him by the arm. "I'll explain it all to you," she whispered. "While Mary deals with Josh, okay?"

Meeting Josh's eyes, Mary could see both the doubt and the hope in them. "Ask me a question," she said, inwardly feeling a sense of déjà-vu. "And I'll ask him."

"Tell him not to ask me any question about those magazines I found in the corncrib," Dale grumbled. "I ain't about to talk about those with ladies in the room."

Mary chuckled.

"What?" Josh demanded.

Taking a deep breath, Mary repeated Dale's words.

"I wasn't going to ask you about those," he shouted to the room. "I'm not sixteen anymore."

Then he froze, eyes wide with shock and looked at Mary. "He really is here, isn't he?"

Mary nodded. "Yes, he can't move on until we figure out what happened to him."

"He's been here, stuck here, since he died?" he asked.

"Yes, he has."

"Jessie used to say she could see him sometimes," he whispered, awe in his voice. "We used to tell her she was nuts."

"Jessie's not nuts," Quinn inserted. "She's just more sensitive than the rest of you."

Josh walked over and sat down on a chair near the desk. "He was murdered."

"Yes, he was. And I think we are close to figuring out who was behind it," Mary said, sitting on the edge of the desk in front of Josh. "So what did you find in the county board minutes?"

"I found…wait! How did you know…?"

"Because I got my own copy from Linda this morning," she said, holding up her envelope. "I just haven't had the chance to read it yet." She looked around her office. "It's been a little crazy here."

"Okay. Well, during all of the meetings prior to the sale of our land, Sawyer was talking up the project," he said. "Saying how the ecological impact reports looked good and how this farm would be a showcase farm and we'd even get international visitors to Freeport because of it."

"So, Sawyer was all for it," Quinn said. "That's not a surprise, considering how much money he made from the deal."

"That's just the thing," Josh continued. "After the sale of our property, when the committee was going to actually vote, Sawyer does a one-eighty. He totally blasts the project, tells the board the impact studies were wrong, that the watershed impact would not only pollute the neighboring farms, but could threaten the city's water supply."

"Yeah, and in those days, whichever way Sawyer Gartner voted on the County Board, the majority followed suit," Stanley added.

"That's exactly what they did," Josh said. "They voted it down."

Mary picked up the pile of papers on her desk and flipped to the last one she'd been looking at. "The sale of the Gartner property was on May 25th," she said. "Josh, do you remember the date for the sale of yours?"

"The same day," he said. "The 25th."

"So, Sawyer's deal was probably contingent on the sale of your land," Mary said.

246

"That's a pretty good motive for murder," Stanley added.

Mary nodded. "Yeah, but the tricky part is proving it," she said, still flipping through the paperwork. Suddenly she smiled. "Well, it looks like we got a break on our side. Josh, why don't you give Jessie a call and have her come over too?"

Chapter Thirty-eight

"So why don't you want your husband to know about this?" Jessie asked as they entered the Lincoln-Douglas building later that evening.

"Plausible deniability," Mary said, as they walked into the elevator together. "He's not responsible for his wife breaking and entering."

Jessie pressed the button for the second floor. "But I work here," she said.

"And if you had asked to see Sawyer Gartner's files from fifteen years ago?" Mary asked.

"They would have told me he is not my client and the information is confidential," she replied with a sigh.

"Yep, breaking and entering," Mary repeated. "It's not only a building, it's a file cabinet."

"Okay," Jessie agreed. "But if we told your husband, he could have kept the cops away."

"The cops won't come down here if we're breaking into a file cabinet," Mary reasoned. "But if a co-worker shows up, well, then, that's another story."

Jessie's hand shook as she tried to put her key into the office lock. "You're not making this any easier," she said.

"How many times have you had to come back here to work on a file?" she asked.

"A few times," Jessie admitted.

"And has anyone questioned you before?"

"No," she said, with a slow calming exhale. "No, you're right. We'll be fine."

She slipped the key into the lock with calm assurance, twisted it and pushed the door open. "Stand here while I disable the security system," she said, moving over to the receptionist's desk and leaning over the side.

Mary heard a few electronic beeps and then Jessie stood up. "We're good," she said. "All disarmed."

"You have a security system at a CPA's office?" Mary asked, a little surprised.

Jessie shrugged. "Well, all of the information here is confidential and someone could go to town with identity theft if they got into the files of our clients."

"So, what's next?"

"Well, let's go to my office and see what we can find on our system," Jessie suggested. "Generally we don't keep files on the system that are older than five years, but we might get lucky."

Ten minutes later, Jessie flopped back against her chair and shook her head. "We did not get lucky," she said. "The Gartner's have been with the firm for over twenty-five years and their accounts are handled by the senior partners."

"So, what does that mean?" Mary asked.

"Well, I was able to hack into their current files," Jessie admitted.

"Good for you!" Mary replied.

Jessie looked at her and shook her head. "I'm supposed to be an honest accountant," she said.

"Okay," Mary said, chewing her lower lip for a moment. "How about…excellent use of incorporating technical skills in a difficult situation?"

Grinning, Jessie nodded. "Much better," she said. "But the bottom line is we don't have the information we need. All of Gartner's online information is only a couple of years old. The older stuff will be kept in the vault in the senior partner section and only they have the combination to it."

"The senior partner section is the hallway I was looking into when I first met you, right?" Mary asked.

"Yes, that's right."

Mary stood up. "Well, come on, I have an old friend who might be able to return a favor."

"What?" Jessie asked, following Mary out of her office and down the hall. "What are you talking about?"

Mary stopped in the reception area and faced Jessie. "So, Josh mentioned to me that you used to think you saw your dad around the house sometimes, after he died," Mary said. "Is that right?"

"Yes," Jessie said, shrugging it off. "I would catch glimpses of him all around the house. But I guess it was just wishful thinking."

"No, you saw him," Mary replied.

She watched one expression after another flit over Jessie's face: hope, doubt, consideration and finally a little bit of healthy fear. "Do you think you see ghosts?" she asked, slowly stepping away from Mary.

Biting back a grin, Mary stepped away from Jessie. "Does this make you feel safer?" she asked. "If you'd like I can climb over the receptionist desk and we can yell at each other."

Jessie stopped moving. "Sorry," she said. "You just kind of freaked me out."

"Yeah, people get freaked out when I talk about things like ghosts and spirits," Mary said. "But not because they don't believe in them. It's usually because they sort of do believe in them, but are afraid to admit it."

251

"It's kind of hard to prove," Jessie said. "Especially when all you see is a quick glance or you just hear his laughter over your shoulder." Her eyes filled with tears. "Or you think he just told you he was proud of you. People think you're kind of nuts."

"I bet it felt good, though," Mary replied. "Hearing him say that."

Jessie wiped her tears away and nodded. "Yeah, it did."

"Okay, well, since your dad is busy tonight…," Mary began.

"What? Busy?"

"Yeah, he's over at Sawyer Gartner's house practicing his haunting skills," Mary said with a grin. "Anyway, since he's not going to show up and help me convince you, like he helped me with Josh earlier this afternoon, I'm going to have to call on someone else to help."

"Someone else?"

"Yes," Mary said with a quick smile. "So, tell me the name of the past senior partner who was a little man, who wore a dark suit and tended to forget where he placed his pencil."

"Mr. Carpenter?" Jessie asked. "He died about two years ago. He was the kindest man in the world, but he was always…"

"Sticking his pencil behind his ear and forgetting where he put it?" Mary finished.

"Yes," Jessie said, a question in her voice. "How did you know?"

"When I was here the other day, he was in the senior partner hall searching for his pencil," she replied. "I pointed it out to him just as you showed up."

Jessie's eyes widened. "When you were tucking your hair behind you ear?" she asked.

Mary nodded.

"That's exactly what I would do when we were in meetings together," Jessie laughed. "His eyes would open wide, he reach up and then he'd wink."

"Exactly," Mary said. "And since he owes both of us, I'm sure he's going to let us into the vault."

"But he's dead," Jessie repeated.

Mary started down the darkened hallway and then turned back to Jessie. "That's even better, because then he won't leave any fingerprints."

Chapter Thirty-nine

"Mr. Carpenter," Mary called as she strolled down the hall. "Mr. Carpenter, I really need your help."

"Mary, really, he's dead," Jessie said, following her into the hall. "I know you're trying to help us, but this is really crazy."

The small man Mary had seen earlier stepped out into the hallway through a doorway at the end of the hall. "Hi, Mr. Carpenter," Mary said. "I'm Mary O'Reilly, thanks for showing up."

Jessie came up behind Mary. "Who are you talking to?" she whispered.

"Mr. Carpenter just stepped out of his office to meet with us," Mary said. "That was his office, wasn't it, at the end of the hall?"

Nodding, Jessie stared into the empty hall. "Yes it was, but Mary, no one is here."

"Mr. Carpenter, do you remember Jessie?" Mary asked.

"I do," the old man said. "One of the brightest accountants we had on staff. Have they made her a senior partner yet?"

Mary turned back to Jessie. "He wants to know if they made you a senior partner yet."

After a burst of astonished laughter, Jessie shook her head. "Okay, I know he's not there if he asked you that question," she said. "They aren't even considering me for that kind of promotion."

Mary turned backed to the ghost. "Did you hear that?" she asked.

Mr. Carpenter stroked his chin with his fingers. "I recommended her two years ago," he said, shaking his head. "Just before I died. Why would they postpone her advancement?"

"He recommended you two years ago," Mary told Jessie. "But he doesn't know why they didn't act on it."

"He did what?" Jessie asked. "Really? He recommended me?"

Nodding, Mary turned back to Mr. Carpenter. "I have a theory to share with you," she said.

"I love theories," he replied with a twinkle in his eyes. "My favorite is the mathematical control theory. Which one do you want to discuss?"

"Well, this theory is not quite mathematical," Mary said. "It's more situational."

"Go right ahead my dear," he said with a smile.

255

"If a certain CPA firm has a long-standing and prestigious client that has something in his files that could prove detrimental if it were discovered," Mary said. "Could that client have enough influence to block the advancement of a junior accountant?"

"Ms. O'Reilly, I believe we are moving from hypothetical theories to actual fact, are we not?" he asked.

Mary smiled and nodded. "Yes, Mr. Carpenter, I believe we are."

"Now, I was a great accountant, but I was never very good at algebra, so could you do away with the 'a plus b equals c' and fill in some names?"

"I would be very happy to do so," she replied. "Your firm's client, Mr. Sawyer Gartner, could have been involved in the murder of Jessie's father. Part of the evidence could potentially be found in his files from about fifteen years ago. If Jessie were to be made partner, she would have had access to those files. Could he be covering his…um, assets?"

Mr. Carpenter shook his head. "Those are very serious allegations," he said.

"Yes, and we have substantial circumstantial evidence to back up this theory," Mary said.

He nodded. "And Jessie, what does she think?"

"Well, I think she believes I'm a little crazy because I'm speaking with you," Mary replied honestly. "But she felt the evidence was strong enough to bring me here to the offices after hours to try to access his file and determine the truth."

"She has a good head on her shoulders," he said. "I don't see her jumping to any rash conclusions."

"I agree with you," Mary said. "What do you suggest?"

He shrugged his shoulders and then smiled slowly. "I say we break into the vault and take a look at those records."

"I think that's a brilliant idea, Mr. Carpenter."

"Follow me," he said.

Jessie watched in amazement as Mary walked further down the hall and the door to the vault room opened before Mary reached it. Moving closer, her jaw dropped as the security code buttons to the vault lit up and within moments, the heavy steel door swung open.

"What did you do?" Jessie asked.

Mary shook her head. "I didn't do anything," she answered. "Mr. Carpenter has faith in your judgment. You did it, not me."

Before Jessie could reply, a black and white cardboard box floated from the depths of the vault and slid onto the top of a conference table in the room. Mary walked over and read the label on the outside. "What a surprise," she said with a smile. "It's Sawyer Gartner's file."

Chapter Forty

Jessie still hadn't made a lot of coherent statements since they had left the CPA offices. "The box just floated," she repeated, shaking her head.

"No, Mr. Carpenter, the ghost, carried it for us," Mary explained again. "And then he put it away. No fingerprints. No breaking and entering. Piece of cake."

"But there was no one there," Jessie said, her voice still on the edge of hysteria.

"Yes, there was," Mary tried again. "But you just couldn't see him."

Jessie shook her head. "I don't believe in ghosts," she informed Mary.

Mary nodded and smiled. "Oh, well, I see what the problem is then," she said. "You just want a logical explanation."

"Yes," Jessie replied. "That's it exactly."

"Okay, how about I'm a trained hypnotist and without your knowledge I hypnotized you and made you see amazing things, like vaults opening and boxes floating, when really nothing like that happened at all."

Jessie exhaled with relief. "Yes, that makes sense."

"The only problem with that explanation is that I'm holding a copy of the files from Sawyer Gartner's folder," she said. "But perhaps that's just a figment of your imagination too."

"You couldn't have just left it there," Jessie said. "You couldn't have just let me believe there was a logical, although farfetched, explanation for everything I've seen tonight."

"No. No I couldn't," Mary said.

"Why not?"

"Because, once we reach the seventh floor and walk into the conference room, your father will be there," Mary explained. "And if you have a believing heart, you might be able to see him. And I think you both would enjoy that."

They walked into the lobby of the Stewart Centre and summoned the elevator. Because it was nearly ten o'clock, the elevator door opened immediately and the women stepped inside. Mary pushed the button for the seventh floor and they were whisked upward.

"Dad will be there?" Jessie whispered hesitantly.

"Yes, he will," Mary said.

260

"What will he look like?"

Mary thought of the broken and bent image of Dale she saw and prayed that the reflection Jessie was able to see was of an earlier time in his life. "I'm not sure what he'll look like," she said. "What I see when I meet a ghost is what I need to see in order to help them. What did you see when you used to see him at your house?"

Tears filled her eyes as she thought back to those rare moments. "I just saw my dad," she replied.

"Then I would guess that's who you'd see tonight too."

The elevator door slid open and they walked down the hall to the big conference room. The room was already filled with people and the smell of pepperoni pizza. "I figured since I made you miss your lunch, I at least owed you some dinner," Josh said as they walked in.

Mary smiled at him. "Thank you, that was very nice."

Abe stood up and walked around the room to meet her. "So, Josh tells me you're trying to find out who killed our dad," he said.

Mary nodded. "That's right."

"That's not what you said when you came to my shop."

"Would you have spoken with me if I had told you what I was doing?" she asked.

He paused for a moment, examining his own feelings, and then shook his head. "No, I would have told you to get the hell out of my shop," he replied.

Mary met his eyes. "Which is kind of what you said anyway."

Abe nodded, embarrassed. "I thought I was protecting my family."

"Yeah, I got that," Mary said. "And so did your dad. He was pretty proud of you for standing up for family like you did."

"He was there?"

"Yeah, he told me you were the most diligent of the kids," she said. "That's why I asked you if you had checked earlier."

"I can't believe dad's been hanging around all this time," he said. "And his murderer has been allowed to walk free."

"Well, let's see if we can't change that," Mary said.

Abe offered her his hand. "Thank you," he said. "For not walking away from us."

"No problem," Mary said, shaking his hand. "I'm glad we're on the same team."

"Me too," he said and then walked back around the room to speak with his brother.

Bradley came up to her carrying a plate and a bowl with a small salad. "Everything okay here?" he asked, glancing over to Abe.

"Oh, yes, everything's fine," Mary said. "Thanks for coming."

"No problem, I'm here to make sure something healthy gets in your system," he said, bending over and giving her a quick kiss. "How'd it go?"

"Great." Mary said, pulling out the file. "It looks like we have motive. How's Clarissa?"

Bradley smiled. "How do you think?" he asked. "She got to spend the night at the Brennans."

"Yeah, I think she's good," Mary said with a smile, and then she turned to the rest of the people in the room to get things started, but saw Quinn approach Jessie. "I think I'm going to start things in a few minutes."

Bradley followed Mary's eyes and nodded. "Good, it will give you a chance to eat something."

On the other side of the room, Jessie watched Quinn approach. Her feet were frozen to the spot, so she swallowed and tried to look away, but Quinn wasn't going to let her get away that easily. He stepped closer and took her hand in his. "It's good to see you," he said softly. "You're looking good."

She smiled shyly and nodded. "You too," she said. "How are you doing?"

"I'm good," he replied. "I've moved up in the bank. I really like banking, you know, helping people."

"You were always good with people," she said. "You know, friendly."

"How are things going with your job?" he asked.

"Great. Just great," she replied, trying to think of something less inane to say. "Oh, Mr. Carpenter said he recommended me for senior partner."

Quinn shook his head. "I thought Mr. Carpenter died two years ago."

Jessie bit her lower lip and pulled her hand from his. "That's right, he did," she said. "But somehow, he was there tonight, at the office. He helped us get the file. I don't understand…"

He took her hand back and smiled at her. "Yeah, neither do I, even when Rosie tried to explain it. But I guess interesting things happen when you work with Mary O'Reilly."

Jessie looked up and met his eyes and saw acceptance, and more, in them. She blushed happily and nodded. "Yes, I guess they do."

Seeing the smile on her face, Mary nudged Bradley. "Looks like things are warming up over there."

"So are you Mary the ghost-helper or Mary the matchmaker?" he asked.

"I think I prefer psychic sleuth," she whispered with a grin.

"What?" he asked.

"I'll tell you later," she replied and then she cleared her throat and turned to the other members in the room. "Okay, I think we ought to get started."

They all gathered around the table: Mary, Bradley, Josh, Abe, Jessie, Quinn, Rosie and Stanley. But Dale was not there yet.

Mary slid the folder across the table to Jessie. "Jessie, Dale's not here yet," she said. "But I think we can start without him. So, why don't you give everyone a brief explanation about what we found in Gartner's file?"

Jessie flipped the folder open and then looked up at the rest of the people seated around the table. "Well, first, the information I'm about to share with you is still confidential," she said. "And because we didn't have a search warrant, we really can't use it in a court of law."

Bradley turned to Mary. "No search warrant?" he asked, one eyebrow lifting.

"Shhhh," Mary whispered. "One of the senior partners gave us the information. So, I was fine."

"Was the partner alive or dead?" Bradley whispered back.

Mary shrugged. "I'm pleading the fifth," she replied with a smile.

"The financial records show that for several years prior to the Maughold project the Gartner farm was running in the red," Jessie said. "The equipment was old, the house had a lien on it from a second and a third mortgage and Sawyer's expenditures outweighed his income."

"I always wondered how he could live so high on the hog," Josh said. "His kids always went to Disneyland; they always had the best clothes and newest electronic games. I just figured Dad was stingy."

Jessie shook his head. "He was so far in debt, there was no way for him to recover," she said. "He was going to lose his farm."

266

Quinn looked across the room to Bradley. "How hard is it for someone outside a bank to find out about someone's financial status?" he asked.

"Well, actually, running a credit report will give you a lot of basic information," he replied. "Debt to income levels. The extra mortgages on the farm. All of those would have been red flags."

"So, I'm an investor looking to start a corporate farm in the Freeport area," Mary suggested. "I know I'm going to have to get approval from the county board and I also know that in rural America corporate farms are not really welcome. So, I find out who's on the county board, which is public information and I run credit checks on all of them to find out which one of them is the most susceptible for a bribe."

"Yeah, that works," Josh says. "But it doesn't explain why our property was pulled into it. They could have just paid Sawyer a bunch of money under the table. He didn't need us."

"But what if it wasn't really about the corporate farm," Quinn suggested. "What if someone at Maughold was looking to make a little money? He approaches a board member with the idea that they buy his property upfront and the deal dies. He gets to buy back his land at current prices and the two split the cash."

"How much land did Sawyer have?" Bradley asked.

"Only 500 acres," Quinn said. "Too small for the corporate farm."

"Which is why your farm was so important," Mary said. "Without your farm, they couldn't make the deal."

"How much money did he make on the deal?" Rosie asked.

"Over eleven million dollars," Jessie said. "And, it's very interesting to note that the year the project fell through." Her voice thickened and she took a deep breath. "The year my dad died, he suddenly had over five million dollars in revenue."

"So we have opportunity, we have motive and we have a financial trail," Bradley said. "All we have to do now is prove it."

Dale appeared behind Josh's chair. "All we gotta do is somehow catch the fox in the chicken coop," he said. "And the fox is running a might scared right now, he thinks he's seeing a ghost."

Jessie's eyes widened as she stared across the room to the spot over her brother's chair. "Dad?" she exclaimed, her eyes wide in astonishment. "Dad you look just like Josh."

Mary smiled and turned to Bradley. "And I think I know how we can do it."

Chapter Forty-one

The driveway that led down to Sawyer's house was gray asphalt and was bordered with tulips and crocuses. Occasionally some statuary of a troll or frog was tucked near a bush or under a tree. It was a very welcoming setting, but Mary doubted the owners would be that welcoming if they understood why she was there.

Parking her car in the circular drive in front of the house, she walked up the steps and knocked on the front door. A moment later, Sawyer Gartner opened the door and scowled. "Can I help you?" he growled in the most unhelpful way.

"Oh, I'm sorry," Mary replied pleasantly. "You probably don't remember me. I'm Mary. We met when I was being shown the house next door."

His frown relaxed into a smile. "I'm sorry," he said apologetically. "Of course, now that you mention it, you do look familiar. I apologize, for my rudeness. I've been a little on edge lately."

Mary bit back the smile as she recalled Dale's stories of haunting Sawyer's house. "Oh, I'm sorry," she lied. "Shall I come back at another time?"

"No, no, come in," he insisted. "What can I do for my potential neighbor?"

Mary came in, but stayed in the front foyer of the house. "I don't want to intrude on your day," she said sheepishly. "But I have an odd question for you. I've tried to speak with the realtor about it, but she just evades my questions. And that makes me even more nervous."

"Nervous about what?" Sawyer asked.

Mary leaned forward slightly and lowered her voice. "Do you know…" she paused.

"Yes?" Sawyer prompted, leaning towards her.

She took a deep breath. "Do you know how the former owner of the house died?" she asked.

Sawyer jumped back as if he'd been scalded. "What? Why would I know that?" he demanded.

Mary shrugged. "Well, because you live next door and you said you were friends," she said simply. "So I thought you must have known."

Sawyer leaned against a door frame and inhaled quickly. "Ah, oh, I'm sorry," he said. "Of course I know. He died in a farming accident. He must have accidentally locked himself into a grain silo when his sons were out harvesting the corn crop. They didn't know he was in there when they emptied the harvest into the top of the silo. He was crushed and suffocated."

"Oh, how awful," Mary said, covering her mouth with her hand. "That had to have been a horrible way to die. Maybe that's why..."

She paused, met his eyes for a moment, and then turned away. "No. Never mind."

"Never mind what?" he asked.

"You're going to think I'm crazy," she said, shaking her head nervously. "I can't believe it myself."

"Believe what?" Sawyer nearly yelled.

She leaned forward again. "I think I've seen him," she whispered. "I mean, I think I've seen his ghost."

"What is he doing?" Sawyer asked.

"Just walking around the house," Mary said. "I've been to the house twice and both times, out of the corner of my eye, I've seen a man."

"What does he look like?" Sawyer asked, his voice shaking slightly.

"He's tall with brown hair, he's wearing a plaid flannel shirt, a pair of overalls and a denim barn coat," she said. "And he's wearing work boots. Does that sound like him?"

Sawyer nodded, his eyes looking past Mary. "Yes," he whispered slowly. "That sounds exactly like him."

"It's so strange," Mary said. "I thought ghosts only came back when they were murdered."

"Where did you hear that?" he asked.

"Oh, well, I read things and watch documentaries," she replied. "And let me tell you, I would hate to be someone a ghost is after."

"Why?" he stammered. "Why is that?"

"Well, if they don't drive you mad," Mary said, lowering her voice dramatically. "They find some way to get even."

Sawyer swallowed. "Good thing," he began, but his voice squeaked and then he cleared it several times. "Good thing he wasn't murdered."

Mary nodded. "Yes, because he doesn't seem like the kind of man I'd want to mess with," she said.

Suddenly a loud crash came from the back of his house. Sawyer looked at her with fear and panic in his eyes.

"Oh, well, I don't need to take up any more of your time," she said, grasping the door and pulling it open. "Thanks for the information."

"Don't you want to stay," he offered urgently. "I can make refreshments."

"No, sorry, gotta go," Mary said, stepping back out of the house. "Have a nice day."

She pulled the door closed on Sawyer's face and swallowed to keep down the laughter that wanted to bubble to the surface. Sawyer Gartner was going to get his just deserts and she was happy to be part of the group that was giving it to him.

Chapter Forty-two

"So, how did it go?" Bradley asked as Mary walked into the house.

"Well, if I had any doubts that Sawyer is our murderer," she said, "his behavior this morning swept them all away. He was very nervous and when Dale knocked over something in his living room, I thought he was going to have a heart attack right there on the spot."

Dale appeared in the room and Mary walked over and put her hand on Bradley's shoulder.

"I dropped his good citizenship award off the mantel," Dale said. "It was given to him the same year he killed me. Just my little way of saying I disagree with the judges."

"Are we all set for tonight?" Mary asked.

"Yes, we're trading the Brennans, they get Clarissa all day today and overnight and we get the whole crew next Friday for pizza and a movie, so they can actually go on a date."

"That sounds like a fair deal," she said. "But the girls get to pick the movie this time."

Bradley nodded. "Okay, but nothing too violent or scary," he said. "The last one you picked even gave me nightmares."

She leaned up and kissed his cheek. "Wimp," she teased.

"I also picked up all of the recording equipment at the station," Bradley said. "Once Josh is wired, all we have to do is get Sawyer to confess."

"What do you want me to do?" Dale asked.

"I want you to watch Mary," Bradley said.

"What?" they both asked in unison.

"Wait, this is my case," she said.

"Yep, and you are carrying my baby," he replied. "Besides, having extra people near the house will only be a disadvantage. Sawyer could see you."

"But, I'm a ghost," Dale said. "I should be in on kill. Um, excuse the pun."

"We need you next to Mary," Bradley explained. "She'll be wired in too and she'll be able to hear everything Sawyer is saying. She can feed Josh information from you. If he asks a question that only you could answer, you have to be there."

Mary and Dale both frowned. "Fine," they grumbled.

Bradley grinned. "Nice to see that both of you are being such grown-ups about this," he teased.

"Okay, so what do we do until then?" Dale asked.

"Well, you could go back and drive Sawyer a little more crazy," Mary suggested. "But don't do too much; we don't want him leaving his house. And I'm going cruising for a ghost."

"Cruising?" Bradley asked.

Mary nodded. "Yeah, wanna come?"

"Sure," he replied. "I haven't gone cruising…come to think of it, I've never gone cruising."

"Me either," she said. "Should be fun."

"Well, while you two go waste gasoline, I'm going to get some real work done," Dale muttered and faded away.

"I like him," Mary said.

"Kind of reminds me of Stanley," Bradley added with a nod. "A lot like Stanley."

Because the weather was so nice, they used the Roadster and Mary let Bradley drive. With the top down and the warm breeze blowing through her hair, Mary relaxed as they headed towards Highway 75 on the north side of town.

"This is really nice," she said. "It's almost like a date."

He looked over at her. "Yeah, but the last time we had a date your mom ended up barricading herself and Clarissa in the basement," he said.

"You sure know how to show a girl a good time," she chuckled. "Well, there was our honeymoon. That was sort of like a date."

Bradley grinned. "If that's what you consider a date, we need to go on a lot more of those," he said and then he paused. "Hey, how many boys did you date before you married me?"

She giggled. "No one, remember, I'm the girl with the big brothers."

"Yeah," he said with a contented sigh. "I really like your brothers."

"So, do you want to go on a date tonight?" she asked. "You know, after we solve a murder and all."

"Sure, where do you want to go?" he asked.

"I know this cute little ice cream parlor," she said. "It's got a jukebox."

"Sold," he said. "And I'm figuring that we are going after hours."

She turned in her seat and smiled at him. "Did you notice that I'm developing a habit of going to places after they're closed?"

"I just figured you were really shy," he replied.

She nodded and sighed. "Yeah, that must be it."

Bradley took the curve on Highway 75 slowly, while Mary scanned the area for any signs of Adam. "Oh, wait," she said, pointing back towards a steep ditch that rolled into a steeper gully. "I think I see him in there."

"Okay, let me turn around and I'll park on the shoulder."

Bradley drove a little further until he found a driveway, turned the Roadster around and then pulled back to the place Mary had spotted the ghost.

"Come on," Mary said, sliding out of the car. "I think I saw him down here."

Bradley hurried around to Mary's side of the car and grabbed her hand. "It's pretty steep here," he said, "Let me help you so you don't fall."

"Bradley, I've been scampering down hills all of my life," she replied, rolling her eyes.

He stepped in front of her, one foot on level ground, the other secured on the grassy incline a few inches below. "Mary, I'm here to take care of ..."

Before he could finish, the foot he thought he'd secured slipped out from under him. Arms windmilling, he started to fall backward. "Oh, no!" he yelled.

Mary jumped forward and grabbed his jacket, pulling on it with all of her might. For a moment she thought he might end of pulling them both down, but finally, she was able to pull him up onto the level surface.

Without another word, Mary walked around him, placed herself on the incline and held out her hand. "You were saying?"

Exhaling loudly, he placed his hand in hers. "I was saying, Mary you've been scampering down hills all of your life," he said.

She grinned. "Exactly."

They were able to climb down the gully without further incident and soon they were walking along the forested banks of a small creek. "He couldn't have gone that far," Mary said. "The trees would have stopped them."

"Well, if you go back more than fifty years ago, a lot of these trees wouldn't have been here," Bradley said.

"Oh, yeah, good point," she agreed.

Mary looked around. It was really a beautiful spot. The creek was shallow and gurgled over and around brown, grey and black river stones that had long since been made smooth by the constant movement of water. The edges of the creek were just beginning to burst with green, as jack-in-the-pulpits, plantain and cattails were pushing out of the brown soil and up towards the sunlight. The air smelled wonderful, a combination of moist clay soil, spring breezes and fresh water. She wished she could bottle it up and bring it home. "We should have brought a picnic lunch," she said.

Bradley dug into his jacket pocket. "I have some lifesavers," he offered.

Mary reached over and chose the green one on top and popped it into her mouth. "Perfect," she said.

Suddenly she heard a noise behind her and turned. Her audible gasp had Bradley reaching for her hand and his exclamation echoed hers. The young man, wearing a letter-sweater from Aquin High School with the year 58 on it, was pushing his way through the vegetation towards them. His head was crushed on one side and mottled blood covered most of his face. "I'm sorry to bother you," he said politely. "But I can't seem to find my girlfriend. My car flipped off the road and I've been searching for her, but I can't find her anywhere."

"Is your girlfriend Erika?" Mary asked. "Erika Arnold?"

A smile wreathed his face. "Yeah, that's her," he said. "Have you seen her?"

Mary nodded. "Yes, I have, she's been looking for you too," she said. "Can you meet her tonight at about ten-thirty at Union Dairy?"

"I sure can," he said, trying to run his hand through his hair, the dirt and dried blood making it impossible to smooth. "I guess I gotta clean up a little if I'm going to see her."

"She will be happy to see you no matter what you look like," Mary said. "She's been waiting for you for a long time."

"Yeah, me too," he replied eagerly. "Gosh, it seems like I've been searching for her for forever."

"We'll see you at ten-thirty, right," Mary said. "If for some reason you can't find it, just think of me and you'll find it right away."

"Are you some kind of genie?" he asked.

Mary smiled. "Yeah, something like that," she said. "See you then."

Chapter Forty-three

Mary was silent as they maneuvered their way up the side of the gully and back to the car. Before he opened her door, Bradley pulled her into his arms and held her tenderly.

"He was so young," she cried softly.

"And now he gets the girl and gets to cross over," Bradley reminded her. "You did your magic again, Mary the genie."

She snuggled into his embrace and leaned against his chest, enjoying the warmth and security of his arms. "Don't you ever wish for a happy ending, just once?" she asked.

He kissed the top of her head. "Darling, they are all happy endings," he said. "We just happen to be sitting on the wrong side of the curtain."

She smiled up at him. "That was the perfect thing to say," she replied. "Thank you."

He opened the car door and she was about to get in when she noticed a small patch of dandelions in a sunny spot near the road. "Oh, would you mind helping me fulfill another promise I made?" she asked.

"Then will you feed me?" he begged.

She laughed out loud. "Yes, I promise."

The house Dr. Springler lived in was a small modest home located in the Willow Lake subdivision just north of Freeport. Bradley drove down the streets named after familiar birds, Robin, Mallard, Swan and Finch, until he finally reached Eagle.

"The house is just down here," Mary said. "In the middle of the block."

Bradley pulled the Roadster into the driveway and Mary hopped out, the small bouquet of dandelions in her hand. "I'll just be a minute," she promised.

She hurried across the lawn and knocked on the front door. A moment later the door was opened and Dr. Springler stood on the other side. "Oh, Mrs. Alden," she said.

"Mary, please," Mary invited. "I'm sorry to bother you at your home, but there was one more thing I needed to do."

Dr. Springler shook her head. "No, you don't have to convince me any longer," she said. "I don't know how you do it, but I believe you have a unique ability to communicate with those who have passed on."

"Dr. Springler," Mary began.

"Karen, please," the other woman offered.

"Karen," Mary said with a smile. "I'm so glad you believe in what happened yesterday. Not for my sake, but for your own. What Brandon was able to do was very unusual and I know he must love you a great deal in order to come back and find you."

Karen nodded and wiped away a tear. "He was right," she said. "I'd hidden away and hardened my heart. His death was so hard on me; I didn't think I could ever survive loving and losing again."

"It is very hard," Mary said. "And no one can understand the pain of losing a child, unless they've had it happen to them. But I know those same loved ones would want us to live our lives to the fullest until the time we can be with them again."

"Well, I'm going to try," Karen said. "I'm going to live and laugh, the way Brandon would expect so if he ever comes looking for me again, I'll be in those places we used to love."

"Speaking of Brandon," Mary said, holding up her bouquet of flowers. "He asked me to deliver these as a favor. He said they were your favorite flower."

Karen took the wilted bouquet and held them to her heart. "We used to pick them all the time," she said, "especially when he got too weak to play in the park. I would push him to a sunny spot and we would sit together and make flower chains with dandelions. He said he liked dandelions because they were brave enough to be flowers where people walked and ran."

Mary smiled. "I never thought of them that way," she said. "But he's right. They don't stay safely in the flower beds; they venture out to lawns and roadsides."

"And they bring joy to others because they're accessible," she said. "You don't think I should plant the whole front yard in dandelions, do you?"

"Well, your neighbors might not be very happy when they all go to seed," Mary laughed. "But I'd make sure there are at least a couple of patches in there, just for a reminder."

Karen stepped down from her doorway and gave Mary a hug, surprising Mary to no end. "Thank you," Karen said, stepping back and taking a deep breath. "I feel like a weight has been lifted off of me. I feel light and…," she closed her eyes for a moment. "Happy. I feel happy."

"Well, actually, it was all Brandon," Mary said. "And since you raised him to be the brilliant young man he is…actually, it's you you should be thanking."

Karen laughed. "Well, before we get even more confused, I'm going to stop while I'm ahead," she said. "I think. Thank you, Mary. I look forward to getting to know you and your family even better."

Mary nodded. "And you still owe me a lunch date at Union Dairy," she said. "Brandon told me about your ice cream tasting combinations and I think you and I have a lot in common."

"That's sounds perfect," she said. "Perhaps next week?"

"That would be great," Mary agreed. "Have a great weekend Karen."

Mary turned and hurried across the lawn to Bradley. "So, how did that go?" he asked.

"Great," she said. "Actually, better than great."

"Well, good," he replied, putting the car in gear and backing out of the driveway.

"So, Bradley," Mary asked. "What would you think about a patch of dandelions in our flower garden?"

Chapter Forty-four

Sawyer Gartner pulled on his chore jacket and grabbed the flashlight from the hook next to the door. Even though the days had started to get longer, it was still dark in the chicken coop and he needed to make sure they were locked in for the night and the coop doors were securely closed against predators. He stepped out onto his back porch and jumped when the door slammed behind him. Turning he stared at the door. "Must have been a draft," he muttered slowly, still eyeing it.

Dale Johnson grinned and glided along Sawyer. "Am I getting to you yet?" he asked.

Sawyer stopped and looked around, but saw nothing and no one. "Who's there?" he called out, sure he had heard someone's voice.

"No one here but us chickens," Dale taunted. "Oh, and the guy you murdered."

The word "murder" hung on the wind and wrapped its way around Sawyer a number of times. "*Murder. Murder. Murder*," the breeze whispered into his ear.

Sweat broke out over his body and his heart began to race. "Don't know what you're talking about," he stammered. "I didn't kill anyone."

He stomped down the porch stairs and, with a determined gait, walked to the corn crib that also housed the chicken coop. He unlatched the long crossbar that secured the door, turned on his flashlight and pulled the door open. Once open, he secured it to another latch attached to the side of the corncrib that held it ajar. Lifting his booted foot, he stepped carefully over the tall threshold and entered the outbuilding.

He had gone no further than five feet with the wooden door slammed shut behind him. Startled, he dropped his flashlight and was plunged into darkness.

"How does is feel?" Dale asked him, whispering into his ear, "To be locked in, all by yourself, in the dark?"

Grabbing a handful of corn, Dale levitated above Sawyer and dropped the pieces of grain on his head. "Remind you of anyone?" he asked.

Shaking his head in terror, Sawyer stumbled back against a wall. "Who the hell is doing this?"

Dale chuckled softly and then opened the corncrib door once again, allowing light to pour inside the building. "Can't get you too worked up," he said softly.

Pulling a red and white kerchief out of his pocket, Sawyer mopped the sweat from his brow and took a couple deep breaths. "Get a hold of yourself," he grumbled. "No such thing as ghosts. Damn girl just got you thinking about it, that's all. Just a loose latch on the door."

He bent over to pick up his flashlight and saw the pieces of corn scattered all around him. Several tiny pieces of dried corn lay on the flashlight case. Staring at the grain, he pulled his hand back, unable to touch them.

"It's a terrible way to die, Sawyer," Dale whispered. "A terrible way to die."

Sawyer's body shook in fear and he stumbled away from the voice and towards the open door. Forget the damn chickens, he had to get out of here.

He ran out of the corncrib into the farmyard. The sun had just set and a silvery purple light cast its glow on the fields and buildings around him.

"Why did you do it?"

Sawyer nearly screamed aloud when the figure stepped out from the shadows surrounding his own grain bin. It was Dale Johnson, he recognized him immediately, even from this distance.

"You're dead," he cried, shaking his head. "You are not here! You are dead."

"You killed me," the figure said, slowly moving further towards Sawyer, but staying in the shadows. "You were my friend. We grew up together. How could you?"

"You don't understand," he pleaded. "Your father, hell even your grandfather, they were penny-pinchers. Couldn't squeeze an extra two cents out of them if they thought there was a cheaper way to do things. Not like my dad who had to have the newest and the best and the most expensive. My legacy was debt."

"You killed me," the ghost repeated. "You took me away from my family."

"I was desperate," he pleaded. "I needed the money from the sale and there was no sale without your property."

"You cheated that company."

"No. He approached me, the vice-president," he said. "He knew I needed money. Somehow he knew and we were going to pull a fast one on the company. No big deal, he told me, the company had insurance for that kind of thing."

He took a deep breath. "We could have all been rich if you had just listened to me," he yelled at the shadow. "If you had just sold your property…"

"You wouldn't have killed me?" the ghost asked wryly. "How long did you plan it?"

"I didn't," he said, lowering his voice. "I didn't plan it. I got a copy of Quinn's letter from the vice-president. The one Quinn wrote telling him that it was a no go with you. He told me I had to make it happen, that he had too much at stake. I had to make you sell."

"So you killed me."

"No!" he screamed, and then he took a deep shuddering breath. "I was just coming over to talk to you… explain to you …convince you. Then you came out of the house and went over to feed the calves. You were so caught up in those animals, you didn't even see me. At first, all I wanted to do was trap you in there, make you listen to me. But then…I don't know, I knew I could talk Josh into selling. Without you around, things would be so much easier."

"So you killed me."

"Yes, dammit, I killed you," he screamed. "I hit you over the head with my old flashlight. I knocked you out and then I closed and locked the door. I cleaned up the buckets, so no one would think to open the door. I killed you! I killed you! Is that what you want?"

"No, I want my dad back, but since that's not going to happen, this is good enough," Josh said, stepping out of the shadows. "But sending you to jail for the rest of your life is going to have to do."

Bradley stepped out from behind a parked truck, his gun drawn and pointed at Sawyer. "Sawyer Gartner, you are under arrest for the murder of Dale

Johnson," he said, as he came towards him. "Please kneel on the ground with your hands on your head."

The cruiser pulled in at the base of the driveway and Mary, Jessie and Abe piled out. Jessie and Abe ran over to Josh and they all embraced. Mary slowly walked towards them and Dale appeared by her side.

"Thank you," he said.

She shrugged. "Josh got him to confess," she said.

He shook his head. "No, I don't think my staying here was as much about finding my murderer as it was about getting my family back together," he said, looked at his children embracing each other. "Look at them. They've found each other again."

"You've got a great family," she said. "You have a lot to be proud of."

He nodded. "Yeah, it took me awhile, but I finally figured out my legacy wasn't the farm, it was my kids."

He paused and looked around. "Well, damn," he said. "I can see that light you were talking about."

"They're going to miss you," she said.

"Yeah, well, tell them I'll be watching over them," he said with a tender smile, as he gazed at his children one more time. "Tell them to be good to each other. And tell them that I love them."

Mary nodded, her throat too tight to speak. "I will," she finally said, tears rolling down her cheeks. "I will."

"And that baby," he said with a grin. "If it's a boy, Dale's an awfully fine name."

Mary chuckled softly. "I agree, but I might let Jessie and Quinn have that one."

"Good idea," he agreed. "Good idea."

He turned, walked towards the open field, and slowly faded away.

Chapter Forty-five

Union Dairy Ice Cream Parlor was closed for the night, the lights were turned off and only the glow of the fluorescents behind the fountain counter and inside the juke box illuminated the store. Mary unlocked the door and she and Bradley slipped inside. Then she turned and locked the door.

"Wait," Bradley said, placing his hand over hers. "Isn't Adam supposed to meet us here?"

Mary looked up at him with a slight grin.

"Oh, yeah, right. Ghost," Bradley said, releasing her hand and shaking his head. "Sometimes I'm a little slow."

She reached over and kissed him. "I think you're doing just great," she said.

"So, what's next?" he whispered, pulling her into his arms.

Looking up at the love in his eyes, Mary felt a wave of wonder rush over her. It hadn't even been a year since they met, both jogging at the park early in the morning, and now her life was totally different. His strength and tenderness, his intelligence and curiosity, and his acceptance of who she was and what she did, had changed her life. And now, together, they had created a tiny miracle.

"Dance with me, Bradley Alden," she said.

Looping his arm around her shoulder, they walked over to the jukebox. Bradley pulled some coins from his pocket and fed them into the machine. "What would you like?" he asked. "You get four songs."

She glanced up at the clock, it was only ten twenty-six; she had four more minutes until Adam was supposed to show up. Leaning forward, she chose the letter and number combinations for her four songs and pressed the play button. In a moment, they heard the whir of the mechanisms and the record plopped down on the turntable. Soon the soulful sounds of Elvis Presley echoed in the quiet room.

Wise men say, only fools rush in. But I can't help, falling in love with you.

Bradley turned Mary into his arms and pulled her close, stepping slowly to the music.

"Perfect song," he whispered, brushing his lips against her ear and making her shudder.

He slowly swayed her into the darkened back room, where there was a little more floor room, and pulled her even closer. Their bodies brushed together and Mary felt the slow melt she always experienced when she was in his arms. She sighed softly and laid her head on his chest, feeling the solid beat of his heart.

Running his hand slowly up her spine, he bent his head closer to her ear. "Take my hand," he sang, his deep voice thrumming through her body. "Take my whole life too."

She looked up and met his eyes, dark with passion. "I love you," she breathed softly.

Tenderly crushing her mouth with his, the dancing stopped and they stood in the middle of the room, wrapped in each other's love while the soft music filled the room.

The record finished and the mechanical noises from the jukebox brought them back to the present. Mary inhaled a deep shuddering breath. "We really need to go dancing more often," she murmured.

Bradley placed quick kiss on her lips. "Yeah, we should," he agreed.

The strains of the Everly Brothers singing *"Whenever I Want You All I Have to Do is Dream"* now filled the room. Bradley lifted one eyebrow. "Time for act two?" he asked.

She nodded. "Yes, hopefully this will bring Erika here. I think it was their song."

Taking Bradley's hand in hers, she led him back to the main area of the ice cream parlor and they both sat at the counter and waited, hand in hand.

Finally, Mary watched as the air around the jukebox thickened and finally Erika appeared. "Hey," she said to Mary. "That your steady?"

Mary nodded. "Yeah, I thought we could double tonight."

"Double?" she asked. "Well, I would, but I didn't bring a date."

"I saw Adam today," Mary said. "And I asked him to meet us here tonight."

Erika's eyes went wide. "You found Adam?" she asked. "Where did you find him?"

Suddenly, the air near the front door wavered and slowly Adam appeared in the restaurant, dressed in his letter-sweater and looking much better than he had earlier that day.

"Wow, what happened to him?" Bradley asked.

"Maybe he's appearing as Erika remembered him," Mary said with a shrug. "He's kind of hunky."

Bradley squeezed her hand lightly. "Hey, don't forget who brought you."

She chuckled and winked at him. "Never."

Adam slowly scanned the room and he stopped and smiled when he saw Erika. "I've been searching for you for a long time," he said.

"They're playing our song," she said shyly.
"We should dance."

He glided over to her and she stepped into his
arms, then slowly they floated around the ice cream
parlor to their song, laughing and talking. Finally the
music stopped and they stepped away from each
other, although, Mary noticed, their hands were still
linked.

"I need to talk to both of you," Mary said.

"Really? Now?" Erika asked. "We've been
waiting to go cruising for the longest time."

She started to fade away. "Wait," Mary
called. "I just wanted you to hear a new song I really
like. You can wait for that, right?"

"Well," Erika hesitated. "We really wanted to
cruise…"

"Aw, come on," Adam said. "She did get us
together."

Erika sighed. "Fine."

The jukebox's mechanisms whirred again and
another record slid onto the turntable. The familiar
opening drum beats of J Frank Wilson and the
Cavaliers "*Last Kiss*" filled the room. The opening
lines had them both staring as the jukebox. When
they heard the lyrics "*I'll never forget the sound that
night, the crying tires, the busting glass, the painful*

299

scream that I heard last" Erika put her hands over her ears and shook her head. "I don't like this song," she screamed. "Stop it! Stop it!"

Bradley jumped up and pulled the plug on the jukebox. The music stopped and the room was silent. Mary came up to him and took his hand and the ghosts reappeared to him. Now he could hear the quiet sobbing from Erika.

"Why don't you want to hear that song?" Mary asked.

Erika shook her head. "I don't know," she cried. "I don't know!"

Adam put his arm around Erika. "Where did you go?" he asked. "After the accident? I searched and searched for you."

"We didn't have an accident," she insisted. "You were late. We didn't go."

"I picked you up," he said, his voice both calm and gentle. "I picked you up on time and we drove out of town. We went up Highway 75 and we were listening to the Everly Brothers on the radio. I told you I loved you…"

"You just looked away for a little while," she said, tears filling her eyes. "You just looked at me when you said you loved me. It wasn't very long."

Adam nodded slowly and turned to Mary. "It was too long, wasn't it?" he asked.

"I'm sorry," she said to the couple. "Adam, you stayed in the car, but Erika, you were thrown from the car. You both..."

"We died," Erika said. "We died and we didn't even get to prove how much we loved each other."

Mary shook her head. "No, you did get to prove it," she said. "You both died over fifty years ago and you have spent those years searching for each other. Adam was searching the crash site for you and you were waiting here for him."

Adam looked at Erika and smiled. "You were always the prettiest girl I'd ever met," he said. "I still love you Erika."

Smiling through her tears, she wrapped her arms around his neck. "I love you too, Adam," she said.

Suddenly the whir of the jukebox echoed in the room and once again *"Whenever I Want You All I Have to Do Is Dream"* started to play. Adam looked down at Erika and pulled her closer, kissing her tenderly. "Want to go cruising?" he asked.

She sighed and leaned her head against his heart. "Forever," she said.

Slowly, the couple swayed to the music, drifting higher into the air until finally they faded away.

Mary wiped a few stray tears from her cheeks and smiled at Bradley, "Great move," she said. "That last song was perfect."

Bradley stepped away and picked up the loose power cord. "Um, Mary, I didn't do it," he said.

Mary shivered and rubbed her arms. "Okay, well now that was spooky."

Chapter Forty-six

Mary sat back in her office chair and stretched. She looked at her desktop calendar. She'd been working out for exactly one week and a day, and she felt a great sense of accomplishment. She put her hands on her still flat abdomen and smiled. "Are you hungry?" she asked her belly. "Oh, you are? And what do you want to eat?"

She stood up and walked over to the refrigerator. On the two bottom shelves were the items Mary had picked up when she was at the store shopping for healthy snacks. There were snap peas, broccoli florets, mini carrots and ranch dip, multi-flavored rice cakes, some high fiber all grain crackers and low fat cheese dip and a couple small bags of fruit. The top shelf was filled with craving foods: chocolate bars, cookies, pastries, cheesecake squares and some left-over sweet and sour chicken.

"Hmmm, what do we want to eat?" she asked herself. "Do we want yucky rice cakes or a delicious Bavarian-cream-filled donut?"

She paused, as if waiting for a response.

"You're right, we worked out really hard this morning. We deserve a donut."

"Um, Mary, are you talking to a ghost?"

The male voice behind her had her dropping the donut back into the package and turning around, closing the refrigerator behind her. Quinn, Jessie, Josh and Abe all stood behind her, watching her with great interest.

"Well, this is slightly embarrassing," she said with a quick grin. "I'll give you a discount on your next haunting if you don't tell Bradley I use our unborn child as a justification to indulge in my cravings."

"I didn't hear anything," Josh said with a grin.

"I'm sure I saw you reaching for…," Abe paused. "What do you got in there that's healthy?"

"Rice cakes," Mary muttered.

"Gross," Abe agreed. "But, I'm sure I saw you reaching for them and not the…"

Mary sighed. "Bavarian-cream-filled Long John."

"Hey, if you need someone to eat it so you're not tempted…," Quinn offered.

Mary shook her head. "Yeah, I don't think so," she said.

"Well, I think you look great," Jessie said. "As a matter of fact, I was going to tell you that I thought you looked too great and you weren't putting on enough weight. You should really be eating some high carb foods, for the baby's sake."

"See, and that's why I like you so much," Mary laughed.

She walked back to her desk and offered them all seats. "So, what can I do for you?" she asked.

"We just wanted to give you some updates," Quinn began. "I contacted the president of Maughold on Monday, they just got back to me to tell me they've arrested the vice president who worked with Sawyer."

"Tell her what else they did," Jessie encouraged.

"They offered me a job," he said. "In Chicago."

"And?" Mary asked.

"I turned them down," he said, grasping Jessie's hand. "I told them I had much better options in Freeport."

Jessie blushed and nodded. "We're, um, dating," she said.

"So, the other thing we all wanted to talk to you about," Josh said. "Were you really interested in buying the house?"

Mary thought about it for a moment. It was a great house with a big backyard and lots of room for a growing family. And then she thought about her current home and her neighborhood. She pictured her neighbors, especially the Brennan family who were going to be descended on her house that very night, and finally shook her head. "No, it's lovely," she said. "But it's not for me right now."

"Great!" Josh said.

"Great?" Mary asked.

"Well, Abe and I have decided to go back into farming," he explained. "Thanks to Quinn."

"The people at Maughold are selling them back their land," Quinn said. "Once I explained the circumstances behind the sale."

"Selling it to them?" Mary asked. "They should give it to them."

"Well, yes, but if they did that it would be admitting the company was in some way complicit with Sawyer's dealings," Quinn explained.

Mary nodded. "Okay, I understand, but did they at least give you a deal?" she asked.

Josh smiled. "Yes, a very good deal."

"So I thought you didn't want to be a farmer," Mary said.

"Well, Josh is going to handle the financials and I'm going to farm," Abe replied. "I always liked that part better."

"So you're going to move back to the house?"

"Well, just until my new house is built," he said. "In about six months."

"Then what?"

"I think in six months or so, I'll be looking for a house," Quinn said, with a loving look at Jessie. "You know, some place to raise a family."

Mary grinned. "Well, wow! Good news all around."

"We also wanted to thank you," Josh said. "All of us. You not only solved our dad's murder, you brought us back together as a family."

"It was my pleasure," Mary said.

"And I have one more surprise," Abe said.

"What?" Josh and Jessie asked.

"This is going to be great," he said, reaching into his pocket and pulling out a photo. "See this cute little heifer?"

Mary looked at the photo of the black and white cow. "Yes?"

"She's the first cow I purchased for our new dairy and I've named her Mary O'Reilly," he said, beaming with pride.

"Oh," Mary replied, trying to muster up a little enthusiasm. "That's…um…lovely. That's really lovely."

She slid the photo back to him across the desk.

"Oh, no, that's your copy," he said. "I want you to be able to look at her anytime you'd like and, of course, you can come out to the farm and check out her progress yourself."

"Well, I would love to do that," she replied, picturing herself wading through manure in a dairy farm. "Really."

"And the best news is that she is already pregnant," he said. "So you both will be delivering at about the same time."

"How adorable," she said. "Me and a cow, maternity twins."

Josh stood up. "Well, we have to get going. We've got meetings scheduled with the bank," he said, extending his hand to Mary. "Thanks again."

Mary shook his hand. "You are so welcome," she said. "Please give my best to your mother."

After a flurry of goodbyes, they left Mary alone in her office looking down on the picture of her namesake. Finally, with a deep sigh, she walked across the room, open the fridge, pulled out a rice cake and bit into it. "Moo!" she said with a sigh.

Chapter Forty-seven

After work, Mary picked up enough pizza to feed the entire Mormon Tabernacle Choir and wondered if it was going to be enough for the Brennan boys, not to mention the rest of them. When she walked into the house she was greeted with a contingency of starving children and a nearly exasperated husband.

"They're like locusts," he said, as he helped her put out the paper plates and napkins. "I kept throwing food at them and it was scary to see how quickly it disappeared."

He looked at the empty bowl that had been brimming with potato chips only a few minutes ago. "By the way, we need to go grocery shopping tomorrow," he said, shaking his head.

Laughing, she opened the cabinet and pulled out another bag of chips. "They are growing boys," she said. "That's just how they eat."

"Scary," he said.

After the food had been devoured, they all sat in the living room to watch a movie. The debate about which movie to watch lasted nearly fifteen minutes, until Mary suggested that they watch something none of them had ever seen before.

"What?" Andy said. "We've pretty much seen everything."

"How about Dracula?" Mary asked.

"We've seen it," David Brennan said.

"The 1931 version of Dracula?" Mary asked.

"Was that one with the real Dracula?" Andy asked.

Grinning, Mary nodded. "Well, it is the one with the original Dracula," she agreed. "And it was filmed using only black and white."

"That's cool," David agreed.

"I don't know," Bradley said. "That was before ratings. They might see something their parents wouldn't want them to see."

"We can see it."

"They won't mind."

"Please!"

Mary bit the inside of her cheek to keep from smiling. "Okay, we'll let you see it," she agreed. "But you have to agree not to tell your parents."

Bradley inserted the movie into the DVD player and then scooped up some of the paper plates. Mary followed with another armful.

"You are brilliant," she said, giving him a quick kiss on the cheek.

"Thanks," he said. "You're not bad yourself."

Arming themselves with several large bowls of popcorn that they distributed around the room, they cuddled together in the loveseat and enjoyed the movie themselves. A quick seventy-five minutes later, they were onto the second part of their double-feature with the 1931 version of Frankenstein. And when Katie and Clifford arrived at ten-thirty, they were all still arguing whether Bela Lugosi or Boris Karloff was scarier.

An hour later, the house was quiet and Mary was snuggling into her pillow, fighting sleep until Bradley joined her in bed. She let her eyes drift closed as she listened to him move around in the bathroom. She awoke a few moments later, listening to the water running in the sink and tried once again to stay awake.

"Honey," she yawned. "You have to hurry, I'm sinking fast."

She started to drift off again and then she felt the weight of someone sitting on the bed next to her. "Finally," she muttered, turning to him.

The scream flew from her mouth before she could stop it and Bradley dashed into the room, a toothbrush still in his mouth. "What?" he demanded.

Not able to form words yet, she slowly reached out her hand in his direction. He ran to her side, grasped her hand and saw what she was looking at.

Sitting on the edge of the bed, no more than two feet away from Mary, were the fleshless decomposing remains of a corpse. The head slowly cocked to one side and hollow eye sockets met her eyes. "Sorry to bother you so late," he said, in a very genteel tone. "But I rather think I might be dead and I was wondering if you could help me."

The End

About the author: Terri Reid lives near Freeport, the home of the Mary O'Reilly Mystery Series, and loves a good ghost story. She lives in a hundred year-old farmhouse complete with its own ghost. She loves hearing from her readers at author@terrireid.com

Other Books by Terri Reid:

Mary O'Reilly Paranormal Mystery Series:

Loose Ends (Book One)

Good Tidings (Book Two)

Never Forgotten (Book Three)

Final Call (Book Four)

Darkness Exposed (Book Five)

Natural Reaction (Book Six)

Secret Hollows (Book Seven)

Broken Promises (Book Eight)

Twisted Paths (Book Nine)

Veiled Passages (Book Ten)

Bumpy Roads (Book Eleven)

PRCD Case Files:

The Ghosts Of New Orleans -A Paranormal Research and Containment Division Case File

Eochaidh:

Legend of the Horseman (Book One)